June Andrea Hanson
SUMMER OF
THE STALLION

ILLUSTRATED BY GLORIA SINGER

MACMILLAN PUBLISHING CO., INC
New York
COLLIER MACMILLAN PUBLISHERS
London

To Anja and Petra
for their love and faith
in Janey

LIBRARY OF CONGRESS CATALOGING IN PUBLICATION DATA

Hanson, June Andrea.
  Summer of the stallion.

  SUMMARY: Twelve-year-old Janey's experiences as
she helps capture and break a wild stallion result in
an altered perception of herself and her relationship
with her grandfather.
  [1. Horses—Fiction. 2. Grandfathers—Fiction]
I. Singer, Gloria, date II. Title.
PZ7.H1987Su   [Fic]   78-24212   ISBN 0-02-742620-3

Contents

A Depot Morning

Whoooo . . . . . . Whooo. It was the whistle-moan of the 6:15 local approaching the railroad crossing. The train stopped with a loud screech, the iron wheels grabbed at the iron tracks. It made me shiver. I pulled my pillow over my head. I'd been sleeping through noise like this since I was a baby. How?

Clink. Clank. Bang. The trainman loaded the milk cans onto the freight car and tossed the empties onto the platform. The train started up again . . . steam hissed. The wheels clacked along the tracks outside my window and faded into the other sounds of the morning.

A robin chirped away out in the Russian olive tree. A rooster crowed from the barnyard across the tracks. I could hear someone poking around in the kitchen. It was probably Daddy making a pot of coffee on the hot plate. He and I were always the first ones up. He wouldn't start the coal stove this morning. It would be too hot. The coal stove made the house unbearably hot in the summer, but there was never enough heat in the winter. The ceilings in the depot were too high and the place wasn't insulated. Daddy said it would take the fires of hell to heat the place when it was twenty degrees below zero with a Montana wind blowing. He had tried to get the railroad to insulate the part of the depot we lived in, but they supplied free coal and thought that was enough.

My bedroom door opened and Daddy poked his head inside. The tuft of gray hair growing out of the top of his bald head was sticking straight up as it did every morning. Sometimes it would be lunchtime before he remembered—or my mother reminded him—to comb it down.

"Daylight in the swamp," he called in a loud whisper. "Last day of school. Summer. Get up."

"*Daddy*. It's too early. The 6:15 just went by," I said as I pulled the covers up over my head.

"Come on, Janey." He walked over and tugged at my foot. "It's a great morning. Get up and walk to the pump house with me. You know I'll only be seeing you on the weekends after today. You'll be so busy riding the range with Grandpa, you'll forget all about me. Besides, I want you to do your packing before school so we can leave for the ranch right after the picnic."

"Oh, all right," I grumbled. I didn't really mind. It would be a good way to get the day going. I was awake anyway. I guess the train woke me because I was excited about the last day of school. I climbed out of bed, brushed my hair out of my face so I could see where I'd dropped my blue jeans the night before. They were too big around the waist. Why did I have to be so skinny? I found my tee-shirt and tennis shoes and headed for the bathroom. When I got to the kitchen, Daddy was sitting drinking his coffee. He had set a cereal bowl and a glass of tomato juice out for me. It was one of our private breakfasts. Just the two of us.

"Eat up, Janey, and we'll get going. Got to fill that water tank," Daddy said.

"But you said you wanted me to pack," I teased. I knew he

mostly just wanted my company this morning. I was going to stay with Grandma and Grandpa at the ranch all summer and even though my little brother Greg would be staying here at the depot, I knew Daddy would miss me.

I ate a bowl of Grape-Nuts quickly and Daddy watched me over the top of his wire-rimmed glasses. We went together through the living room and the passengers' waiting room out onto the platform. I had to squinch my eyes together for a moment until I was used to the sun. It bounced off the steel surface of the tracks like rays from Flash Gordon's gun.

Daddy took my hand and we walked along beside the tracks. I thought the sunflowers in the ditch seemed to be nodding good morning. The milkweed were laden with clusters of pink flowers, palest silver-dust pink. Shiny bits of dew sparkled from the fuzzy tufts of the fox-tail grass.

Daddy sighed. "It's going to be a good year, Janey. We've been getting some nice spring rains and good warm days in between. Good for the crops. Plenty of hay. Might even have some to sell and be able to buy a few more head of cattle. The herd is building up pretty well. Maybe, in four or five years, the ranch will be bringing in enough income to support us. Then I'll retire and we can live there for good. No more weekends."

The ranch was Daddy's dream. He had told me that when he was out of work during the depression he had sworn he'd have his own land and security someday. He had worked as a railroad depot agent and saved his money for many years before he met Mom and got married. He bought the ranch soon after I was born, but kept his job with the railroad so he could build up the ranch. In the meantime, Mom's parents lived on it and took care of things.

"You know, Janey, we own the prettiest ranch in south-

eastern Montana. Having the Tongue River running through it like a big wet ribbon and those wild blue-stem hay meadows and all. It makes me happy that you love it, too. I'm going to need you out there. Someone in the family should be able to ride the place. I wish I were better on a horse, but I started too late. You learn all you can from Henry. I don't approve of many of the things he does, but he knows cattle and horses, and he can teach you a lot. Of course you'll have to go to college, too. I want you to be a well-educated rancher. Think of reading *The Hound of the Baskervilles* or *Macbeth* on a cold winter night and listening to coyotes howling over on the big bluff across the river. . . ." Daddy smiled thinking about it.

I squeezed his hand. He was the best dad even if he was so much older than my friends' fathers. He told me wonderful stories and treated me like a friend. Always had, ever since I was little. He took Greg and me swimming and skating and read to us, talked to us about important things like money and politics. Some people thought he was wrong to involve us in things like that. I remember how annoyed Mrs. Rogers, the president of the Republican Club, had been when Daddy and I showed up at the polls on voting day with my old stuffed elephant that I'd named Dewey. She didn't think it was funny at all, but Daddy and I had laughed a lot.

At the pump house Daddy took out the grease can. He oiled the armature of the huge engine that pumped water from the well high up into the wooden water tower so the locomotives could fill their tanks to make steam. Then he turned the switch and cranked the engine to start it. He didn't have to do this too often anymore, because there were more diesel engines than steam locomotives now. Daddy told me he thought they might take down the depot when he retired. The railroad didn't need these small stations anymore. I didn't want to believe him. The depot was home. I looked down the tracks. There it sat; a long, gray building with the windowed-office part sticking out onto the platform. My bedroom was right next to the office. Sometimes the phone would ring late at night and Daddy would go to answer it. It would be an emergency of some kind. I would get up and put on my robe and go into the office. Daddy would talk on the phone about things like "hot box" or "derailment." He would call up the section crew and telegraph messages to the depot agent down the line. If it was cold out, he would get the office stove going and make a pot of coffee. I had always thought living in the depot much more interesting than living in a real house.

The water tower loomed high above us on the right. It was like a prehistoric bird—its four steel legs rising out of huge cement feet; the body, the wooden tank. The big pipe, which was held up by pulleys and lowered to fill the water tanks of the trains, was the long neck, and the funnel on the end, the beak. When I was little I had been afraid of it. I thought it was alive because once I had heard *coooo, cooooo* when I walked by it. I had grabbed Daddy's leg and started to cry. He had tried to explain that it was the pigeons who lived in the girders under the tank making the noise, but I didn't believe him, and for years I had clung tightly to his hand whenever we passed the water tank.

Daddy came out of the pump house and walked around to the pipe to see if the flow had begun. Then we started back toward the depot. We didn't feel like talking on the way back. The pale yellow blossoms of the sweet clover and the soft yellow throat of a meadowlark perched on the fence post were the same exact color, the color of Grandma's freshly churned butter. It was a good morning.

"Well, where did you two go so early?" Mom asked as we entered the kitchen.

"Just up to the pump house," I answered.

My towheaded, almost toothless brother, Greg, was sitting at the table eating Wheaties. He loved Wheaties because of the picture of the baseball player on the front. Greg was eight-and-a-half. He was in the third grade. We were both in the same room at school. We got along okay. I could still beat him up.

"Hey, Janey," Greg taunted. "What position are you going to play in the game today?"

"I don't know, Fatso." He was just trying to make me mad. He knew I was terrible at baseball. He loved to play and was pretty good for his age.

Mom turned from the sink. "Stop that, now, Janey. Greg is not fat." I scowled. He *was* chubby. "Now get yourself some breakfast and be quick," she snapped.

"I had some cereal with Daddy already," I answered. "I've got to pack now." Mom sure wasn't in a good mood. She put her hands on her hips. They left wet marks on her flowered skirt. "How do you propose to get packed for the summer in fifteen minutes?"

"I'm only taking some shirts and jeans and shorts. Maybe one dress for going to town. Besides, if I need other stuff, you and Daddy will be coming out on weekends. I'd better hurry, though," I said and left the kitchen.

In my room I quickly put some clothes in my suitcase, then some comic books, a book I had borrowed for the summer from my teacher called *Children of the Covered Wagon*, and a set of jacks. There wouldn't be anyone to play with on the ranch, but I could practice my jacks so I would be good when school started again next fall. I couldn't think of anything else I wanted, so I closed the suitcase and put it in the office beside Daddy's desk. The big electric office clock said 8:10. The bus would be coming in about five minutes if Joe, the driver, got started on time today. I ran back to the kitchen. Mom was sitting at the table having her coffee. Greg was playing with a little car on the table.

"I'm all packed and my suitcase is in the office, Daddy. Come on, Greg. The bus will be here in a minute and you know Joe doesn't wait for anybody."

"*So?* I don't need you to tell me," he answered like a brat.

"What is wrong with you, Greg?" I yelled.

"You think you're so smart, don't you, Janey, such a big deal. 'I already had my cereal and now I have to pack,' " he mimicked. "You think you're so important, going to stay on the ranch."

"You could come, too, you know." I was trying to be reasonable, but I wanted to sock him.

"I don't even want to, so there. There's nobody to play with on the ranch but you, and who wants to. Besides, you always get to ride the horses because you're Grandpa's pet. I'm glad you're going."

He ran out of the kitchen, before I could get near him.

"For crying out loud. I have enough to do today without listening to you two carry on like crazy crows. Get out, now," Mother said loudly.

Greg made me furious. As I stormed out the back door Daddy told me I'd better hurry or I'd miss the bus. I yelled back that I was going to walk because I couldn't stand to ride on the same bus with Greg. Daddy laughed.

I felt tight and angry as I walked up the little hill and on to the main road. The big cottonwoods along the side were drooping with millions of small, green, round pods. The apple trees in the Halls' orchard were loaded with blossoms, promising some good apple stealing in the fall.

As I watched a robin hopping from branch to branch, his orange breast like a lighted match in the snow of blossoms, I thought about what Greg had said. He was right. I was Grandpa's pet. Ever since that time with Pal and the bobcat Grandpa had treated me differently from the way he treated Greg and my cousins. I was pretty little at the time—six or seven. I had been wandering around in the big cottonwoods on the ranch with my dog. Pal had been my best friend then. Daddy got him for me when I was a baby and we had grown up together. He was a big German Shepherd and Airedale mix. Very big. He took good care of me. Daddy and Mother didn't worry about my going off by myself if Pal was along. This time, though, Pal had jumped a bobcat. Grandpa had been out riding and heard the fight. He came galloping up to rescue Pal. Grandpa made me hold his horse while he tried to shoot the bobcat. I did it—took care of the horse for him even though I was terrified. Afterwards, I heard Grandpa tell Grandma, "Janey had pluck." Then he had started to teach me to ride and would take me with him when he worked the cattle. I liked it. You never knew what might happen when you rode with Grandpa.

I hurried on. My best friend, Diane, was sitting on the dark green steps in front of the school. The building only had two rooms; one for the first through sixth grades and one for the seventh and eighth grades. This was our last year in the room for the lower grades.

"Come on, Janey," Diane shouted as soon as she saw me coming. The bell rang and I ran the rest of the way.

Sad Start

Our classroom was in pandemonium. All the kids were jumping up and down. Two of the fourth-grade boys were trying
to fly paper airplanes out the window and Miss Vohm was
banging a yardstick against the side of her desk. You could
hardly hear it. Finally, she got everyone to sit down for
announcements about the game and the track meet. We stood
for the pledge to the flag and sat down again.

Miss Vohm smiled. "I just want to say that it has been a
wonderful year for me, despite the frog in my lunch box and
those April Fools' Day pranks. You are a lively bunch. I've
learned a lot from you and hope you have learned something
from me."

It was the usual end-of-school speech. The class was starting to fidget. Miss Vohm continued. "I hope each of you will
enjoy your summer and return ready to work in the fall. I
will be teaching here again, as most of you already know.
I am pleased to announce that all of the sixth grade will pass
on to Mrs. Terry's room."

Two of the boys in our class groaned. We all laughed. Mrs.
Terry was a very strict teacher. She wore funny black dresses
and dark stockings. She wasn't like Miss Vohm, who had only
been out of Teacher's College for two years and wore saddle

shoes and bobby sox and went on dates with Joe, the bus driver. None of us were supposed to know, but we had seen them together at the movies in Forsyth.

"Now I shall call your names and I would like each of you to tell the class and me what you plan to do this summer, just a few words. Then come up to the desk and pick up your report card. I'll start with the first grade. Gary Beal."

Gary Beal was a big seven-year-old who had failed the first grade once. He missed school a lot. He stood up and said, "I'm going to irrigate sugar beets and beat up on my sister."

Everyone laughed. He walked up to the teacher's desk. She handed him a report card. He opened it right there—in front of everyone. He smiled a big, toothy smile. "I passed!"

We all applauded.

Delbert Smith said, "Miss Vohm, you gave him the wrong report card."

Everyone wanted to say something funny after that. It got very silly. Almost all of them were going to help on their farms. The Covvaruz twins were going to Mexico to visit their grandmother, and John Yellowfeather said he was going to the Cheyenne Reservation for a rodeo. I said I was going to work on the ranch, but no one was listening by the time it was my turn.

The noise in the room was awful. Miss Vohm told us we could go out to the baseball field and wait for her to come and assign captains.

"Hey, Janey," Delbert Smith called. "I hope you ain't on my team."

I was so embarrassed. "Shut up, Delbert," I said, and tried to sound like I didn't care. I wished I didn't have to be on anybody's team. I couldn't catch and I couldn't bat. The only thing I could do was run the bases. I was a good runner. At least there was a track meet, too, so I could be good at something.

Miss Vohm picked Tommy and Diane for captains. I almost fainted! Diane wasn't much better at baseball than me.

They chose teams and I was picked third from last; only two first-grade girls were behind me. I was humiliated. If I had been a captain, I would have chosen Diane at least second or third, even though she wasn't any good.

The game began. I struck out all three times at bat. Our team won in the end, but I didn't enjoy it. My little brother hit a triple.

"All right," Miss Vohm shouted. "Time for the girls' relay. Janey, would you run into the schoolhouse and get the batons?"

I ran all the way. I was glad to be picked to do something. I decided to enter everything this year—the relay, the hundred-yard dash, the fifty-yard dash and the high jump. I loved to high jump. Sometimes I came to the schoolyard at night and on weekends to practice by myself. I pretended I was an antelope. Antelope were the ballerinas of the prairie. They ran with small bounds as though they were poised on toe shoes with muscles tensed and ready for the next leap. They could clear fences the way I stepped over a stick. I would see a picture of an antelope in my mind and run when it ran and jump when it jumped. I would go up off the ground, over the pole, and land in the soft dirt of the high-jump pit below just as the antelope touched the buffalo grass. A lot of the kids wanted to know how to high jump like I did. I showed them my scissor kick and my start, but I never told them about the antelope.

We went to the pasture just outside the schoolyard fence where we ran the relays. There weren't any cattle there, just a little bit of cactus and sagebrush. I took my place beside a clump of sage. The sun was high now, close to noon. Parents were arriving for the picnic. I looked back at my team standing in their positions. My stomach did a funny slow wiggle with a flop at the end. The first runner in our line was a tiny first grader. She stood nervously banging the baton against her legs. There was a sharp blast of the whistle. I looked back. Nell, the first grader, was running pretty fast for a little girl. The other team had the edge, though.

Our second runner almost captured the distance but Patsy, a slow second grader, was next. She stumbled and fell. We lost a lot of time. Our next runner was terrific. Her arms and legs were going like pistons on the water-pump engine. She gained back some distance and suddenly it was my turn. I saw Miss Vohm ahead with the white handkerchief. I heard a hawk scream as it circled overhead. "Run, run!" it cawed. I ran. Each foot pounded "Run!" I ran.

I saw Miss Vohm's arm floating downward holding the handkerchief, but I didn't know who had won. Then my whole team was jumping up and down and hugging me. We won!

Miss Vohm congratulated our team and gave us each blue ribbons, which were attached to big shiny gold stars.

They had the boys' relay, and Delbert Smith was on the losing team. Served him right.

It was time to high jump. They started with the pole very low for the little kids. Ribbons would be given for the best jumpers in the first and second grades, and for the best in the third, fourth, fifth and sixth grades, but we would all jump together. We got two tries. I looked around the schoolyard between my jumps. A lot of the parents were there but mine hadn't come yet.

The pole was getting higher now. It was almost to the

notch where I liked to start. Some of the seventh and eighth graders had drifted over to watch. It made me nervous. Quite a few of the girls were eliminated on this turn. They raised the bar again. It was my turn and I was about to start my approach when I saw Dad's 1942 Chevrolet pickup drive inside the schoolyard fence. I waved. I wanted them to see me jump. I wiggled back and forth from foot to foot, as I liked to do, and ran toward the pole. Just as I got there, even with the pole, I saw the antelope leap off the earth. I hadn't been thinking about the antelope. It was just there in my mind, and I was easily over the pole. A few of my friends cheered. It wasn't really high enough for cheers.

I went over to see Mom and Daddy.

"Janey, you looked like a deer," Mom said.

I smiled and said, "I am a d-e-a-r. You know that."

She laughed. She looked pretty. Her blonde hair was washed and shiny. She had on a neat white sleeveless blouse and her blue-and-white checked skirt. Sometimes she tended to get too fancy, but today she was just right. Daddy had on his pleated, pin-striped suit pants and a white shirt. I wished he wouldn't wear those pants, but whenever I said anything he laughed and told me I should be proud; they were tailor-made twenty years ago and of such good stuff he'd have them for another twenty. If only he would wear jeans like the other fathers.

It was my turn to high jump again. There were only four of us left. I made my jump on the first try. Now it was just Geraldine Cross and me. Mom and Daddy and Greg were standing together on the sidelines. I looked at the pole. It was chest-high now. I closed my eyes for a moment, then ran. I made it. Geraldine ran and jumped. She ticked the pole, but it didn't fall down. They raised it again. I stood in place and wiggled back and forth. I started running and stopped. My feet didn't feel right. I went back to my starting position. Most of the school was watching now. It was scary. I wiggled my feet again and closed my eyes until I saw the antelope clearly this time. I ran and jumped when the antelope jumped. I landed in the soft dirt and looked back. The pole was swinging . . . but it stayed up.

"Yeah, Janey!" came a yell on my right. I looked over and Greg was grinning at me through his missing front teeth.

Geraldine missed both tries. I had another blue ribbon! Mom and Daddy both hugged me. The fifty-yard dash was starting right away so I didn't really have time to enjoy the victory.

We walked out to the road for the fifty-yard dash. It was dirt, not gravel, and there wasn't any traffic on it. Miss Vohm blew the starting whistle and right away I was way out in front. Three blue ribbons for sure! Then, Plunk! My toe smashed against a stone. It threw me off balance. My arms began to go every-which-way. I saw the road flying up at me, then I felt myself rolling off onto the prickly buffalo grass at the edge. I tried to get right back up and hold my lead, but my foot sent a sharp pain through my leg. I tried not to cry, but I wanted that blue ribbon.

I heard Daddy say, "That was some fall. You looked as though you were caught in a tornado with your arms, legs and what-all getting whipped in four directions at once."

My foot was beginning to swell above my tennis shoe. I squeezed my eyes and lips as tightly closed as they would go, but the tears and the cry came from way down and pushed through.

Daddy put his arms around me and said, "I'm going to get the pickup and I'll take you right into Forsyth and we'll have the doctor look at that foot."

"My foot is all right," I cried. "I want to run the hundred-yard dash."

"Not this time," said Daddy. "That ankle is growing like a puffball after a rain. Let's get some ice for the swelling."

A crowd had gathered around me. I saw Diane.

"Is Janey going to be okay, Mr. Anderson?" she asked. He nodded. Greg came running up.

"Janey, what happened? You were way ahead. You should have won by a mile. Geraldine won and she wasn't even close to you," he shouted.

I bit my lip.

Daddy smiled. "You were running a fine race, honey, but maybe trying a little too hard, running a little too fast. When something got in your path it threw you. Maybe you just have to learn to pace yourself."

I nodded, but I didn't want to talk about it anymore.

Daddy, Mom and Miss Vohm agreed I had a sprain and did not need to go to the doctor or have an X-ray. The races continued while I sat in a chair by the big picnic table with a towel full of ice around my foot.

When the races were over, everyone lined up at the table with paper plates. There were dishes of potato salad and jello salad and carrot-and-raisin salad; stacks of homemade biscuits and buns sat beside mounds of butter in pans of ice. Roasters full of fried chicken were sandwiched between platters of sliced ham and roast beef. There were two card tables full of desserts, cakes, cookies and brownies. Final-Day picnics were always feasts. Diane got a plate for me.

After lunch came the baseball game between the parents and the seventh and eighth graders. Daddy picked me up before I could protest and carried me to the edge of the baseball field. I felt silly. Some of the older girls were giggling into their hands and I knew everyone was looking at us.

The seventh- and eighth-grade boys were moving around in front of me planning their strategy. The parents' team had gone out to the field. Bobbie Winters called to the first batter, Vonnie Foster. "Hit it over to left, Vonnie. That crazy old nut is playing shortstop. He's so old he can't bend down and his pants are so baggy, he'll trip if he runs."

I froze. Several of the kids around Bobby laughed and cheered in agreement. I looked out into the field. There was Daddy, standing at the shortstop's position, squinting through his glasses into the sun. I wanted to kick that stupid Bobby Winters and break his shins and bloody his nose and pull his hair out by the roots. I wanted to tell Daddy to get off that field immediately and to change his clothes. I wanted to leave this place; beat up everyone and get away!

When Diane came over I told her my foot was hurting and asked her to help me to the pickup so I could lie down until the game was over.

I put my head down on the driver's pillow under the steering wheel and closed my eyes, making everything dark and tight. I felt like not being me anymore. I wanted to go to the ranch, now. There were no stupid Bobbie Winterses or Delbert Smiths out there. I could hear chains of the swings clank against the swing poles. I stayed in my darkness and fell asleep.

"Well, sleepyhead. Time to go." It was Daddy. "Game's over and we're off to the ranch. Do you want to sit up front or in the back where you can lie down on the sleeping bag?"

Greg was in the back.

"In front."

Mom climbed in the front, too. Everyone was leaving the

schoolyard. Cars and pickups were filtering out the gate, one by one. I saw Diane standing near her parents' Oldsmobile waving to me. I turned and waved as Daddy backed up and drove toward the gate.

We rode along in silence for a while, past the sugar beet fields and dairy barns of the irrigated river valley and onto the higher, drier plateau with miles and miles of wheat fields. As we rounded the curving road into the pine hills, the tight feeling inside me dropped away. I didn't even know who had won the game and I didn't care. We drove into Miles City, past the swimming lake and through the neon signs of the hardware store, the Range Rider's Bar and the Liberty Theater. I bumped Daddy in the ribs with my elbow as we neared the Penguin Home-Made Ice Cream Parlor.

"Nope, not tonight. You had enough treats today at the picnic."

"But my ankle is hurting and I know some chocolate ice cream would make it better," I whined.

"Hum. First time you've mentioned it. Funny how it started hurting a block from the Penguin."

Mom laughed. She had been quiet all during the ride. Greg began knocking on the back window and pointing toward the Penguin. Daddy stuck to his decision and shook his head. Greg stuck his tongue out. Daddy laughed and we drove on out of town.

The sun was setting and the sky had a pink glow near the horizon which became lavender higher up. The sunset was so big; I didn't know why, but I felt a little sad.

As we turned off the highway onto the Tongue River Road, Mom took a deep breath and, looking down at her hands, said, "Andy, please don't say anything about the lease money. Until Sunday, anyway. What is done is done, and if you bring it up now, the weekend will be spoiled. You know how Dad is. It is never a strict business deal with him. He takes everything personally."

Daddy was silent. Finally, he said, "Dammit, Lenore. You know he really messed me up this time. That lease money was due yesterday. I had the deal all set to buy that new bull. I was counting on the money. Damned embarrassing to have to renege on the deal. What was I supposed to tell the breeder? My father-in-law couldn't pay his lease money because he gave his youngest daughter a loan for a new Buick? Sounds good, doesn't it?"

"I know how you feel, but you know by now that he does things like this. There is nothing more to be done by making a scene. You need him on the ranch right now, and he and Mom need the place to live. I'm asking you not to say anything."

Grandpa and Daddy were always fighting over ranch business. Grandpa said Daddy didn't know anything about ranching and Daddy said that Grandpa was unreliable. I didn't know why there was so much trouble all the time, I just wished they could get along.

The road wound around the river valley, past several ranches and up over the big, rugged cactus-covered sandstone hill, which was now orange with flames from the setting sun. This was my favorite part of the trip. From the top of this hill you could see the prairie to the west; just grass and sage and cactus, reaching and reaching. In the east there was a green band. This was the stretch of cottonwood trees and willows which grew next to the river. Not far from this green strip, a couple of miles off the main road, was the big white ranch house with the four-pillared porch and the gabled roof. Sometimes Daddy stopped here and silently enjoyed the view. Then he would put the pickup in low gear and we would slowly go down the long hill toward our mailbox. It was a small barrel painted white and nailed to a tall white box. Hanging from an iron bar which arced over the barrel was a piece of plywood with **A6** burned into it. That was our brand and the name of our ranch. The **A6** of the Tongue River Stage. That was our address. I liked it . . . Tongue River Stage. It sounded like the olden times. Made me think of cowboys and stagecoaches and galloping horses.

We turned onto the dirt road at the mailbox and stopped for the gate. The first gate was a wooden one which swung on wagon wheel axles. Greg jumped from the back and ran to open it. We drove through. Watching Greg fasten it, then run and jump into the pickup again, I remembered what a good feeling it was to be able to open gates when you were a little kid.

We were greeted at the second gate by the dogs, Pal and Heinie. Heinie was a small, frisky wire-haired terrier. He belonged to Grandpa. He was nice, but Pal was mine. I was so glad to see Pal. A few years ago a farmer who lived near the depot said Pal was bothering his sheep. He threatened to shoot him. Daddy said the farmer was crazy, but he didn't want to take any chances, so we brought Pal to live at the ranch. I missed him, but he was a lot safer out here. Freer, too. He chased skunks, prairie dogs, rabbits, raccoons.

The dogs followed the pickup, barking and jumping up at the windows. Pal was very excited to see us. As we drove into the yard and around to the back of the house, Grandma opened the screen door and waved. She came down the steps. As soon as Daddy stopped the car, Greg was bouncing toward her with Heinie jumping up on him at every step. Mom got out and I moved over to the door. I gingerly stepped down. My ankle was swollen, but I was surprised that it didn't hurt as much as it had before.

"Where's Grandpa?" I said. "I have to tell him about my blue ribbons!" I saw Daddy give Mom a look over his glasses and was sorry I'd asked. I couldn't look at Daddy then, and I bent over and made a fuss about Pal. He walked happily beside me, licking my hand. Grandma hugged Greg, then me.

"Henry is up milking," she said. "Come on in. Janey, did you bring your suitcase? Land sakes, child, why are you walking as though you'd been stepped on by that fool cow, Pansy?"

"I sprained my ankle during the fifty-yard dash, Grandma," I said, and then hurried on, "But I won blue ribbons in the girls' relay and the high jump. I would have won the fifty-yard dash, too, except I fell. . . ."

"You should have seen her, Marie," Daddy cut in. "She ran like a fast pony heading for the barn."

"I hit a triple in the baseball game, Grandma. I really did." Greg shouted, trying to get some attention, too.

We went into the house through the coatroom to the kitchen. The house smelled of fresh bread. The big wood stove was going and Grandma had a stew on in a big kettle. I didn't like stew, but it smelled good. I was hungry. The picnic and school seemed far away. I looked around the familiar kitchen. The table covered with red-and-white checked oilcloth sat in the middle of the room, with a chair at each end and benches on the sides. I couldn't help it, I was so glad to be here.

"Sit down," Grandma said. "Henry will be here in a minute or two. Sit down and tell me about the last day of school."

"I'd rather talk about the beginning of summer," I said.

Rain-and Mushrooms

The weekend went by quickly. Mom and Grandma visited and cooked. They weeded the vegetable garden Grandma had planted. I wanted to ride, but my ankle was still sore, so Greg and I played with the barn cat's new kittens. We went down to the willows by the river and built a house. We cut away the lower twigs and branches in a clump of willows and twisted the upper branches together to make a roof. It was fun. Greg and I didn't fight at all. Grandpa and Daddy did repair work on the fence down around the alfalfa field. They seemed to get along okay. I wished we could all stay at the ranch and that it would always be like this.

On Sunday afternoon when Daddy and Grandpa came back from fencing, Daddy told Mom and Greg to get ready to go. He said he'd decided not to stay for supper and thought they should drive those pine hill curves before dark. We all went to say good-by at the pickup. All except Grandpa. He walked up to the corrals and went into the barn. I guess Daddy must have said something about the lease money, after all.

Daddy came over to me and swept me up against his chest. He squeezed me so hard I could feel the buttons of his shirt pressing against my rib bones.

"Be good, Janey, and remember whose girl you are. I sure envy you. Learn all you can about ranching. Maybe next summer we can make you the foreman, and someday you and I will run the place ourselves." He kissed me and put me down.

Mom told me to help as much as I could. "We'll see you in a week to help celebrate your birthday, anyway," she said. I had almost forgotten. I would be twelve years old on Friday!

Grandma and I waved until the pickup turned the bend by the river.

"Chore time, Janey," Grandma said. "Let's see. How about you getting the eggs and I'll bring in some water and put out some supper for us."

I got the lard pail from the pantry and went back across the yard to the coop. The chickens were coming in to roost for the night. When I walked over to the nests they clucked and fussed a bit. The nests were like rows of birdhouses fastened to the wall. There were three rows, one above the other, with ten nests in each row. The bottom row was easy. I could see into the nests and simply reach in and get eggs where there were some. The middle row wasn't too bad, because I could see in if I stood on tiptoe, but the top row was too high. I couldn't see in the nests at all. I just reached into each one and felt for the eggs. If there was a chicken trying to set on the nest to hatch out chicks, I would put my hand right into the feathers and it was spooky. Sometimes a setting hen would peck at my hand or fly out of the nest at me. It could scare you. I held my breath when I checked the top row. Tonight the nests were clear, but there weren't too many eggs.

When I got back to the house Grandpa had returned with the milk. Grandma was straining it through a clean white dishtowel. When she finished she took my egg pail.

"Seems like there should be more. Those hens must be hiding their eggs again. They want to set all over the place this time of year." She went into the pantry with the eggs and milk.

Grandpa sat down in a chair near the cookstove and took out his Bull Durham sack. I loved to watch him roll his own cigarettes. He carefully extracted a thin white cigarette paper and poured a line of tobacco into its folded center from the cloth bag. He held the gathering string at the top in his teeth and pulled the bag closed. Then he opened his mouth and let the bag drop into his shirt pocket. Now he ran the tip of his tongue over the side of the paper with the glue on it and twirled the paper securely around the tobacco. He squeezed the wet edge down onto the roll, twirled one end of the roll into a twist so no tobacco would fall out, took a big wooden match out of his pocket and made one sharp stroke of the match against the rivet on the back pocket of his pants. The match flared and he lit the cigarette. He tossed the match onto the shiny black surface of the cookstove where it flickered and went out. Grandpa sat there in the evening light, gray curls of cigarette smoke rolling up beside his weathered brown cheeks and white hair. He was silent, staring.

It was funny about Grandpa. He was tough. I'd seen him take the head right off a coiled rattlesnake with a fast spin of a lariat. He was an old-time cowboy. He stood for no nonsense. He frightened me, but I liked to ride and do things with him. It was exciting. I had to do everything he told me just right or he got mad, but the things I did with Grandpa were fantastic adventures. Sometimes he even told me I'd done a good job and I knew he meant it.

Grandma returned from the pantry. "Henry, how about lighting the lamp. It's getting dark. Probably going to rain. Can't see to get supper."

Grandma was talking too fast. I knew she wanted to get supper over with and put me to bed before Grandpa started swearing about Daddy. It was always the same. I hated to hear it. I didn't know what to say. Daddy was only trying to help Grandpa by having him on the ranch. Grandpa was too old to cowboy for other ranchers, and he seemed to go from job to job in town. But Grandpa thought Daddy was a dude and that *he* was doing *Daddy* the favor, running his ranch for free and all. I didn't know who was right. I loved them both and wished they would be friends.

I sat very still, pretending not to notice Grandpa's silence. He was like a bull looking for something red when he was in this mood. I didn't want to attract his attention.

Grandma tried to fill in. "Well, Janey. What shall we plan for tomorrow. If it does rain we can do the baking. Otherwise, it might be a good time to hook up the wagon and go over to the line shack on the other side of the river and pick up that chicken wire. We're going to need it soon to put up some pens for the new chicks. I don't want them running all over the prairie and getting picked up by the hawks. What do you think, Henry?"

"You know damn well that river is too high to take a wagon across now. Right in the middle of spring rise. The wagon bed would be floatin' and draggin' the team with it ten feet from the bank," Grandpa replied sharply.

Grandma pretended not to notice his tone. She placed a plate of cold fried chicken and some home-baked bread on the table. "You're right. I suppose we can't hop across the river this time of year," she said.

"Oh, Janey, I guess I'm not used to having you here yet. I forgot the milk."

"I'll get it, Grandma."

I jumped up and went into the pantry, glad to have an excuse to leave the room at the moment.

When I got back to the kitchen, Grandpa was just going out the back door. Grandma sat with me while I ate two pieces of chicken and drank my milk.

"We'll stack these dishes. I'll do them in the morning. Let's get you washed up. There's some hot water in the tea kettle. You take that out to the washroom and pour a little in the basin. I'm sure there is enough cold water in the bucket to cool it off. You can wash that river mud off your elbows before you go up to bed."

I did as Grandma told me and went back to the kitchen. "Grandma, I have to go to the toilet. Should I take the flashlight?" I asked, hoping she would offer to come with me. She did.

We passed Grandpa, who was sitting on the porch steps smoking and staring. There was thunder way off to the north. We started down the path to the outhouse. I didn't like to come to the toilet alone at night. Once Grandpa had to kill a rattlesnake there.

Grandpa wasn't on the steps when we got back to the house.

"Henry must have gone to bed. We'd better go too. You trot on up and I'll come and say good night."

She handed me the kerosene lamp and told me to be careful carrying it up the stairs. I used two hands. It was heavy.

I undressed and climbed into my bed. The window was

open. I could hear thunder and the rushing of the river as it carried the melted snow, from the hills, downstream. Grandma came in and sat on my bed.

"It's good to have you here again, Janey," she said as she smoothed my hair. "Grandpa feels the same way, too, but he is having one of his moods tonight. Don't want you to think it has anything to do with you, though. He's been telling me about all the work he is going to have you do this summer. He's counting on you and you know how particular he is about his help. I've had to put a damper on some of his ideas, of course. He forgets that you aren't one of those tough Martin boys who were brought up in a corral and act like it. He'll be more like himself before you know it, so don't you worry." She kissed me, blew out the lamp and left the room.

I was glad she told me that. I felt better. There was a big rumble of thunder, then I heard the first few pats of rain on the porch roof outside my window. Then a few more. Soon there was a steady pup, pup, pup, pup on the roof. It was coming straight down and there was very little wind, so I could leave my window open. The rain on the roof was the coziest sound in the world.

I awoke to the same pup, pup, pup. The sky was aluminum gray. I smelled pancakes and was in the kitchen in no time. Grandma was pouring batter onto the griddle and the kitchen was steamy from the heat of the big Majestic range and the cool humidity of this late May rain. Grandpa entered the kitchen as I did. He had come from outside and had on a slicker which was dripping on the floor. His boots were muddy.

"It's raining to beat the band out there. Looks like a general. Have to get the weather report on the radio. If this keeps up all day we won't be able to get the old Plymouth out to the gate. Won't be able to get any supplies before Wednesday or Thursday."

"We can use the rain," Grandma said, "but I hope it breaks so we can get into town. We need most everything. We're low on flour. That means no bread, no pancakes . . . almost out of sugar, too. Well, sit down and eat up. We can't save these pancakes for hard times."

As soon as he finished eating, Grandpa moved over to a chair by the stove to have a second cup of coffee.

"Henry, how about saddling Blue and having Janey ride out to get the mail?" Grandma asked suddenly.

I was dying to go for a ride—even if it was just old Blue and only as far as the mailbox. My ankle was fine, now. And I felt funny in the kitchen.

"Okay," Grandpa said as he stood and stretched. "I'll do it now and then I'm going up to the shed and see if I can fix that broken gear on the hay stacker." He put on his slicker and went out.

Soon he came back down from the barn with Blue all saddled and ready. I climbed up on the big horse. It wasn't easy to mount him, he was so tall. I put my left foot in the stirrup and hung onto the saddle horn as I pushed off with the right foot to get off the ground. Then I had to lean, belly first, into the saddle while I switched my whole body around to get the right leg over. Blue was just too big, a gray-blue workhorse that Grandpa had saddle-broken because he was so smart around cattle. Sometimes when Grandpa had complimented me on my wrangling, the credit really belonged to Blue. He knew when a cow was about to break away and he would move up beside her before she finished thinking about it. But he wasn't very fast or beautiful and I wished I had a saddle horse of my own.

I headed out through the rain toward the main road. I decided to cut across the prairie rather than take the road and have to open the gates.

The dogs came with me. Pal jumped a rabbit in a bunch of greasewood and chased it until it ran into a hole in the ground by a fence post. I saw a few early cactus blossoms, their red-orange centers filled with raindrops, and some white gumbo roses that drooped on their thin stems from the weight of the rain.

When I reached the mailbox I pulled Blue up close and reached in and got the mail without dismounting. I put it in an oilcloth bag Grandpa had tied to the saddle, and turned toward the house. I'd taken my time riding out here, wanting to get away from the tension in the kitchen, but now I was wet and chilled. I trotted back. Blue moved along even though it was slippery. He wanted to get back to the barn. We made good time.

That afternoon Grandma and I made bread. The rain went pounding on. The kitchen stove warmed the room and soon the aroma of the bread made my mouth water. When it came out of the oven, Grandma put out butter and we had hot fresh bread and milk. The fire crackled. Grandpa took a nap. Full and drowsy, I curled up in the big chair beside the stove to read my book. Soon I fell asleep, too. Grandma woke me when it was time to get the eggs. Grandpa had gone to the barn long before to unsaddle Blue and get the cows for milking. The gray day turned light purple as evening came on. Grandma lit the lamps, then fixed us scrambled eggs and stewed tomatoes from a can for supper. I went to bed early. The rain made me so sleepy.

Tuesday was Monday. Gray and rainy. I wanted to do something. I put on my slicker and went down by the river.

The rain and spring thaw had brought the river up over its banks. It was backing up into the slough. I saw a big snapping turtle sitting on a log. There were some fresh raccoon tracks leading up into a hole on the bank of the river. The dogs were with me and they poked around the hole some, but they weren't too interested. I guess the rain probably washed away some of the scent. I wandered up to the barn. Grandpa was in the hayloft fixing a pulley for lifting and lowering hay. I followed him around for a while. He didn't talk to me, but he wasn't cranky. I finally went back to the house and played solitaire until chore time.

At supper, Grandpa said, "Whether it rains or not tomorrow, I've got to go to the upper pasture and check on those two heifers who are ready to calve. First calves, and I want to see them."

I gulped. "Can I go with you, Grandpa?"

"No. I want to ride hard and I don't want to worry about you and old Blue slipping in the gumbo."

I stared down at my food. I wasn't hungry anymore.

Wednesday was gloomy. The rain had stopped, but the sky was still gray and heavy, like a dirty, wet canvas draped over the prairie. Grandpa left after breakfast. Grandma got out her mending and began sewing on buttons and patching elbows of Grandpa's shirts. It was boring. I could do that at home.

"Grandma," I said apologetically. "Do you have any ideas about what I can do?"

She put down her patching and looked at me.

"Let me see. . . ." She thought for a minute. "Why, thank you for asking. We can go out to the sheep shed and see if there are any mushrooms. It so seldom rains like this out here that I forget. But when it gets this wet there's a place back in the corner of the shed where big field mushrooms come cropping out like lily pads on a pond. Big and delicious."

In the corner of the pasture was a large lean-to built of pine poles. The roof was made of bundles of straw tied to the pole frame. The floor of the sheep shed was layers of straw and manure. Grandma started turning over pieces of the straw with her boot. She tossed several pieces to the side. She stopped and bent over. I went to see what she was looking at.

"Our timing is perfect, Janey. Look at this."

She showed me a mushroom growing beneath the straw. It was about three inches high and at least three inches wide. She picked it and handed it to me. The top was a pale brown, like coffee with a lot of cream. Smooth. Its underside was pink-brown and textured like the nose of a new calf. The mushroom was beautiful. I stared at it until Grandma laughed at me.

"Come on. Where there is one, there are many."

We began to turn the straw, carefully. We had a bucketful in no time. Grandma took off her scarf, and we filled that with mushrooms, too, and we went back to the house.

We were planning to give Grandpa a pan of mushrooms fried in butter. Just then he came galloping up on Smoky, the white horse he rode most often. He tied Smoky to the wheelbarrow handle and came into the house in a huff.

"What time is it, Marie?" he asked as he went to the shelf by the window and took out some writing paper and a pen.

"Only about twelve or twelve-thirty. You got back fast. Something wrong? Did you find the heifers?" she asked.

"I didn't even get to see the heifers. That stallion of Gilmore's damned near got me in the ribs with a kick. I'm writing him now and giving him two weeks to get that horse out of here. Got to get this in the mail today. What time does that mailman come back from up the river?"

"About one-thirty or two," Grandma answered.

"Well, I'm getting this letter to him. This has gone on long enough." He addressed and stamped the envelope, left the kitchen, mounted Smoky and headed for the mailbox. We never showed him the mushrooms.

The stallion was a big brown-red horse with a blond mane and tail. He had a white-lightning streak running from his forehead to his nose. He wasn't our horse. He belonged to a rancher from Wyoming who had bought him at auction as a colt and boarded him on our ranch until he could haul him down to Wyoming. Three years had gone by and the spindly-legged colt had grown up running loose in the upper pasture. Now he was a nuisance, or more like a danger. He had banded together three mares and would not let other male horses into the pasture, gelded or not. He had run at Grandpa and me when we were riding one weekend last fall, but Grandpa had been able to chase him off. He must have gotten worse.

When Grandpa returned, the rain started again. The yard was eroded by small rivers which led into lake-puddles wherever there was a low spot. The chickens who had ventured out of their coop during the morning were caught in the new downpour. They were wet and silly looking as they tried to find cover under benches. One foolish hen was standing under the pump handle which was only about two inches wide. I laughed as I watched her maneuvering, trying to keep dry. At last she moved on across the yard toward the coop.

For dinner that night Grandma fried up the mushrooms.

They were wonderful. Grandpa had three helpings and admitted the rain had some advantages.

Tilting his chair back from the table he said, "I'm going to ride up there again tomorrow and find those heifers."

"But aren't you afraid of the stallion?" I asked.

"Hah! Afraid of a horse?" he snorted. Then he looked at me for a moment. "I think maybe you should come with me. One of us can keep the horse busy while the other finds the heifers. Today he had me. I couldn't go anywhere without him snorting, kicking and chasing."

Grandma looked at him and frowned. "But Henry, Janey hasn't done much riding this year, just a little on weekends. Don't you think that's a big order?"

"Janey can ride just fine. I only need someone to go up by the reservoir and get a look at the heifers. I'll decoy the stallion. You want to go, don't you, Janey? Or are you afraid you'll be too saddlesore to celebrate your birthday?" Grandpa added, smiling.

Grandma smiled too, shaking her head. "You know, honey, I don't want you to be disappointed, but your mom and dad may not be able to get through for your birthday after all."

"That's okay. I don't care," I said, trying to sound grown-up. "Being stranded is kind of an adventure. Besides," I grinned at Grandpa, "if they can't make it, then it won't matter so much if I get sore riding tomorrow."

Grandpa winked at me and reached for his tobacco. Summer had finally begun!

Surprises

Grandpa's call awakened me.

"Get on down here. We got to get started."

I hurried into my clothes and down to the kitchen. Grandma was talking: "Now you watch crossing that river, Henry. High as it is, and with junk floating in it . . . I wish you would let it go for a day or two. The radio says it is likely to clear by tomorrow afternoon. Might even stop raining today. That means the river will be down by Sunday."

"I have to check on those heifers now, Marie. I'm taking some antiseptic to doctor 'em if they need it. They ain't goin' to wait for the rain to stop to calve. Besides, Janey will be on Blue. That old horse is so big he can practically walk across during the spring rise. Let's get to it."

Grandpa and I put on our slickers and headed for the barn. It was still dripping but it wasn't coming down now. Blue and Smoky were all saddled and standing in their stalls. I walked into Blue's stall and unwrapped the reins from the snubbing ring hanging on the wall above the manger, backed him out of his stall and out of the barn. We mounted up and rode to the lower river crossing where the river was wide and less deep.

Grandpa stopped and looked upstream. There were willow

branches and big hunks of river grass floating down, but no big logs that we could see.

"We'll be out in that muddy mess in a minute," he said. "You are going to have to swim that horse, but just hang on. Tie your reins together and wrap them around the horn. Wrap your legs around the horn and put your hands on top of it and hang on." He smiled at me.

I tried to smile back, but my mouth did some jerky nervous thing instead.

The horses entered the water. Smoky went first. I watched the water mark rise on his gray-white legs. The water was belly-deep in no time. Smoky made a lunge. His head went up and the water churned around his chest. He was swimming. Grandpa sat astride the saddle with his feet draped around the horn. The water was almost coming over the saddle seat.

I felt Blue lunge forward. I looked down at the brown, angry swirls of current surrounding us. I felt dizzy. I clenched my hands around the saddle horn and tried to look at the bank on the other side. I could swim if I fell off, I knew I could swim. "I can swim," I said out loud to myself, but the words and confidence were carried away in the noise of the rushing current. I closed my eyes and felt the thumping of my heart against my ribs. It seemed a school year before I felt Blue's hooves hit the gravelly bottom again. I opened my eyes. Smoky and Grandpa were up on the bank. The white of Smoky's haunches was stained brown all the way up to his tail. I pulled up on the bank beside Grandpa.

"Wasn't bad now, was it? Feels like one of them carnival rides at the fair, and you don't even have to pay a quarter," he laughed.

I giggled my relief. We rode on. The sky was deep blue-gray, like the back of a pigeon. It looked like it might start raining again. The horses walked briskly in the wet grass. I heard the chatter of magpies in the distance. They didn't know enough to come out of the rain, I thought, then smiled. Neither did we.

Grandpa pointed out the bristly back of a porcupine chewing on the bark of a chokecherry tree. Good thing the dogs weren't with us. Pal and Heinie had been filled with quills many times, but they had never learned to leave the porcupines alone.

Grandpa and I reached the gate for the upper pasture in good time. He opened it and we rode through.

"I hope we can get all the way up to the reservoir without even seein' that stallion, but if he comes our way, I'll keep him busy and you ride straight up to the reservoir and look for them heifers. Their calves will be brand new, the only two new ones in this pasture. You won't be able to miss them. Just check around. See if they look good. You know, not sickly . . . head hangin' down or wild-eyed."

We had almost reached the reservoir when there was a whinny to our right. There, standing about fifty yards away on the crest of a small rise, was the stallion. He watched us as we rode toward a small bunch of cattle we had spotted on the other side of the reservoir. I remembered him as a colt. He had been kept in the corrals for a while after branding. He was the first colt we had on the ranch. I used to sneak up to the corral and feed him fresh carrots from the garden. I remembered the feel of his velvet muzzle nestling into my hand for a piece of carrot. The stallion trotted toward us.

"You get up there and find the heifers," Grandpa ordered as he kicked Smoky and trotted to meet the stallion. Blue and I took off toward the reservoir. I looked over once to see what was happening. The big red horse was standing pawing the gumbo as Grandpa sat on Smoky, not five yards away, watching. I turned back toward the cows.

I found one of the cows with no trouble. She stood by the reservoir with a new calf standing under her. All four legs were spread wide for support and the calf had her nose in her mother's bag, going after her lunch. There were two older cows with big calves and another young cow with no calf and a big milk bag. She didn't look pregnant. Maybe her calf was sleeping where I couldn't see it. I rode slowly around the bunch. No sign of it. I looked over to Grandpa. He had his lariat out and was swinging it in a wide circle. The stallion was galloping back and forth in front of him.

Where was that calf? A little to the north was a niche in a hill and a couple of cedar trees. Sometimes cows left their calves in places like that when they were grazing or going for water nearby. I kicked Blue and we trotted over. I circled the closest cedar tree and found nothing. I was heading for the second when I saw the brown and white hide of a calf lying beside the dark green of a greasewood bush. I rode right up to it. It didn't move. The calf was dead. I couldn't tell how long. The body was stiff and the ribs were sticking out.

My face wrinkled up. I felt the same way as I had when the neighbors' dog was hit by a train. My throat began to hurt and I wished I could run to Daddy as I had then.

"Janey! What did you find?" Grandpa yelled as he galloped toward me.

"One cow and her calf are fine, but look here."

He rode up and looked where I was pointing. "Too bad. Nice little calf, too. How'd the mother look? Never mind. We'll ride by her on our way out. The stallion must have decided that we didn't want his mares and he left to go join them. I'd like to get out of here before he decides to come back."

He rode off toward the bunch without another glance at the dead calf. I followed numbly.

"The cow is fine. She'll have better luck next year," he said as we rode around the cattle. "Come on!" He kicked Smoky and we were off at a gallop, mud flying behind the horses' hooves. We didn't stop until we reached the gate. On the other side of the gate we slowed.

"I'll be glad to hear from Gilmore so's we can get that horse out of here. Damned nuisance."

We rode on toward the river crossing in silence. A few drops began to fall. Grandpa didn't even pause on the bank this time. He urged Smoky right into the water. Before I had time to think about it, I was swinging my feet up over the horn and Blue was rolling from side to side as his legs moved under me. I clung more tightly to the horn and to Blue's mane, too. We were out of the river and trotting up to the barn before I loosened my grip. Grandpa told me to get on down to the house and dry off. He'd unsaddle the horses and rub them down and be there as soon as he could.

Grandma had the stove going and she fussed over me, getting me into dry clothes and finding out what had happened. I told her we had to swim the horses and pretended it was easy. When I told her about the dead calf, she said nothing, but I saw her frown.

Grandpa came down from the barn for lunch. As we ate, he said, "Janey rides about as well as she did last year. She liked crossing the river so much that she closed her eyes so's she could enjoy it more." He winked.

"The water was making me dizzy," I said quickly.

Grandma came to my rescue: "All that swirling does just that. I feel that way sometimes in the buckboard."

"We lost one of the calves," Grandpa continued. "I knew there was something wrong up there. Just had a feelin'. Did you get the weather report, Marie?"

"Yes. It's supposed to clear by tomorrow afternoon. Should be sunny on the weekend," she answered.

For a moment my hopes of Mom and Daddy getting here for my birthday were fired, but I knew they couldn't possibly get through, since the main road was washed out. There was the same cold drizzle coming down. I wondered if it would be sunny tomorrow, and if I would be different when I was twelve.

My birthday was the same color as every other day this week had been. Drippy gray. I went downstairs.

Grandma met me at the doorway to the kitchen singing "Happy Birthday." She clapped her hands together and said, "Now I've been looking over the supplies. There isn't enough flour to make bread, but there is just enough for a cake. We'll get some more of those mushrooms and have a little feast in honor of my favorite helper's twelfth birthday."

She was so enthusiastic, I had to cheer up. It was like the pioneer days when people made do without stores and cars.

"Grandma?" I asked hesitantly.

"Yes?"

"Just one thing. Do we have to have chicken again?"

We had had chicken or eggs almost every day since I came to the ranch because that was all we had without going to town.

"I'll see what I can do. It isn't like being at the depot

where you can run down to the general store for a fresh pork chop. But I'll see what I can do."

Grandpa came into the kitchen from the porch. "Why, I think she looks older, don't you, Marie?"

Grandma said of course and told him to finish his work early today because we were having a party. "One problem, though," she said. "The guest of honor does not want to have chicken."

"We'll see what we can do about that," Grandpa said as he left the house.

Grandma and I went on another mushroom hunt and returned with two pails this time. Grandma fired up the stove while I peeled and washed the mushrooms. She brought out the flour, sugar, eggs, butter and milk, and began measuring and mixing. Grandma never had to use a recipe book for anything. She poured the batter she made into two round cake tins and popped them into the oven.

"Now you go out and cut some wild roses for the table, Miss Jane. Pick anything else which strikes your fancy, too, but don't bring me any wild onions."

I giggled, remembering the time my cousin and I had gathered wild onions for a whole afternoon and brought them in and put them in the ice chest thinking Grandma would be happy to have them. All the milk and butter in the ice chest had to be thrown to the chickens and dogs because it tasted just like the onions smelled.

I gathered roses and some Queen Anne's lace and took them back to Grandma. She put the flowers in her best china vase, the one with peacocks painted on it, and put them in the center of the table in the dining room. There was a fire in the stove, and the big round oak table with the claw feet was spread with the lace tablecloth and set with the good dishes from the china closet in the corner. Grandma had even used the wine glasses with the flowers engraved on them. It was beautiful.

The cakes were cooling on the breadboard in the kitchen. There was the smell of something roasting in the oven.

"What's that smell?" I asked.

"That's for me to know and you to find out. Now go upstairs and get yourself ready for this party."

I ran upstairs and put on the only skirt I had brought with me and my favorite blue blouse with the tulips embroidered on the collar. I brushed my hair and looked in the mirror hanging over the chest. I went back downstairs.

Grandma was in a flowered dress and Grandpa was sitting in his chair by the stove in a clean shirt. This was a real party!

"Close your eyes, Janey," Grandma shouted.

I did and she took me by the shoulders and led me into the dining room. "Open your eyes!"

"*Ooh!*" I gasped. It was beautiful. The table was lit by two big candles on either side of the cake which was piled high with whipped cream and had rose blossoms sprinkled on top. I turned to Grandma and gave her the biggest hug and kiss.

She told Grandpa and me to sit down and eat before it got cold. She removed the covers from two of her fancy silver casserole dishes. One dish had a heaping pile of fried mushrooms and the other was filled with pieces of meat which had been dipped in egg batter and baked. I helped myself to some.

"What is this? It's delicious."

"Ask Grandpa. He's the shopper," Grandma said.

"What is it, Grandpa?"

"I got to think up a good name for it," he said.

I had three pieces of meat and three helpings of mushrooms.

Grandpa said, "You're going to have to go water the sheep shed when the rain stops so's we can keep up with our appetite for mushrooms."

We finished eating and I asked for some cake. It looked so good.

"Not yet," Grandma said. "Just sit still while I clear."

She left the room with our plates. Grandpa pulled out his Bull Durham and started to roll a cigarette. Grandma returned, holding a package wrapped in white butcher paper with a single wild rose lying across it.

"A present? Where did it come from? What is it?" I looked at her in such disbelief she began to laugh.

"Well, open it!"

I did. In the package was a white peasant blouse with delicate lace sewed about the neck and sleeves, and a bright yellow skirt with two big pockets in front with J's embroidered on them. "Oh, Grandma, where did you get the material? When did you make it?"

"Don't you recognize any of it?" she replied.

I looked again, but was puzzled.

"The blouse is some of that nice new sheet that got hooked on the springs of our bed and ripped. The lace is from an old petticoat of your mother's and the skirt is one of the curtains from the room your parents use. Your mother wants to paint the room and change the curtains, so I just used them in advance."

They were wonderful presents.

I turned to Grandpa. "Now will you tell me what we just ate?"

"Back in the old days, we called it the prairie staple," Grandpa answered.

"But what is it?"

"Rabbit," he said.

I gulped.

"Say, how about some cake before the whipped cream makes it all soggy," said Grandma quickly.

Decision

Saturday was sunny. Grandpa went to check the washouts in the road and Grandma and I went down to the garden to drain it. With the hoe and the shovel, we made passages so the water trapped in the low spots could drain out into the grass before the new ferns of carrots and the tiny bean plants drowned.

When Grandpa came back from inspecting the road to the mailbox, he said there were three big washouts and we would have to work on them if we wanted to get to town on Monday.

The three of us worked all afternoon and most of the next day. It was hard work. We had to haul straw and rocks to fill the washes after we drained them. All the hauling was done with the wheel barrow because Grandpa said the team and wagon would make bad ruts and it would be harder to get out with the car. By Sunday night my hands were blistered and I ached all over from pushing the wheel barrow and lifting rocks.

On Monday morning Grandpa said we could try the road. We dressed quickly. I wanted to wear my birthday presents, but was afraid I'd have to help push if the car got stuck. I didn't want to get them muddy. I wore my jeans—the only clean pair I had left.

We piled into the Plymouth. Grandma locked the dogs in the barn so they couldn't follow the car. We started down the road. Grandpa kept the car in first gear and went slowly through the puddles. A couple of times the wheels slid, but grabbed before we hit the ditch.

When we reached the biggest washout, the one we had tried to fix yesterday, no one talked. The front wheels rolled onto the straw and mud we had packed into the hole. You could feel them sink. We began to slide toward the ditch on the left. Grandpa turned the wheel to the right and gave it some more gas. We moved forward, away from the ditch. That was the worst part. Now we could make it to the main road. What a relief. We all began to talk.

"It's too early for the mail, Janey," Grandma said, noticing my anxious look at the mailbox. Then she went over the shopping list with Grandpa.

I sat in the back and looked out the window while I decided what kind of candy bar I would buy for myself with the money Daddy had given me.

We drove down Main Street and went right to Sawyer's Food Store. Grandma went inside to shop while Grandpa went across the street to talk to the man at the seed store. I went in with Grandma and got my candy bar, then went and sat on the steps outside to eat it.

Usually when we came to town I liked to look in the stores on Main Street, but today I hoped we would go right back. I wanted to see if anything had come in the mail for me. The grocery boy brought out four big boxes for Grandma and put them in the trunk. Grandma sent me across the street to get

Grandpa. He was talking with the seed man about the damage the rain had done to the crops up north.

We drove toward the main road. Grandpa said, "I think I'll stop for a beer at the Range Riders."

Grandma didn't say anything. I knew she didn't want to sit around while he had a beer. Often he got to talking with the cowboys and was gone for over an hour. Grandma wouldn't put her foot inside the bar because she said it was a "rough house," so we had to wait in the car or walk about town.

Finally Grandma spoke: "Henry, I think we should get back and get the mail. There might be something there from Gilmore telling you when he will pick up the stallion. Why, he could be coming any day now. You're going to have to get someone to help you bring the horse in. Probably that young Stanley can do it, but you'll have to go up to his place and ask him."

Grandpa stopped for a red light. He didn't want to pass up his time at the Range Riders, but I could tell he knew Grandma was talking sense about the horse and Stanley. He drove ahead on the green without speaking and pulled into a parking place in front of the bar.

"I'll be right back," he said as he got out of the car.

Grandma was staring straight ahead. I watched the people going by on the street. Grandma and I were both surprised to see Grandpa returning in about ten minutes.

He climbed into the driver's seat and said, "Thought I might find Stanley in there, but the bartender says he hasn't been in since the rain."

He placed a brown paper bag on the seat between him and Grandma. "Hang on to this, Marie, so it doesn't spill while I'm getting us back on the road."

Grandma hated drinking in the car about as much as she hated bars, but she didn't say anything.

We drove out of town, passed the funeral home and the radio station. Before long we were down the big hill and pulling up to the mailbox. A big box was propped against the bottom of it. I could barely wait for the car to stop.

"Looks like that box of seeds we ordered came," Grandpa said.

I looked at him with my mouth wide open. I was speechless with disappointment. Then I realized he was teasing me again. I jumped from the car and grabbed the box. It was addressed to me. I started tugging at the string around the package and tearing at the paper, too.

Grandma said, "Get your knife and cut that string before she rips her fingers, Henry. Slow down, Janey."

Grandpa teased me more by taking out his pocket knife and opening it slowly. He pretended to examine the blade in the sunlight. At last he cut the string around the box. I tore off the outer paper and ripped open the box to find two smaller boxes wrapped in gift paper; the kind with flowers and "Happy Birthday" written on it. I ripped that off while Grandma protested. Inside the package were three books I had wanted for a long time: *My Friend Flicka, Thunderhead* and *The Call of the Wild*. I hugged them. . . if only I had had them during the big rain. I picked up the other box.

"Be careful of that paper," Grandma cautioned.

I tried but I couldn't help but tear it a little as I hurried to see what was inside.

"Oh," I sighed. I had wanted these for at least four months. Ever since they had put them in the window at the General Store. They were the most beautiful pair of cowboy boots; shiny black with red and yellow flowers stitched in the tops.

I had dropped a lot of hints, but I never thought I would get them.

"Look! Look!" I yelled.

Grandpa could not stop teasing me. "Now you not only will *be* a dude, you'll look like one, too."

"Henry!" Grandma reprimanded. "Best wait until we have a few more sunny days, Janey, before you put them on. You don't want to muddy that shine right away."

Grandma and Grandpa sat down in the car to read the mail.

"Well, Janey. Your mother says they won't be able to get here this next weekend either because the auditor is coming to the depot and your father is very busy getting ready. She says she hopes you won't feel like an orphan and that you aren't running wild out here."

Then Grandpa looked up from the letter he was reading. "Marie, you sure had the situation pegged. This is from Gilmore. He says he will be here on Saturday to load up the stallion. Says he wants the horse for sure, and he will pay extra for having it in the corral when he arrives. Guess that means we better head on up to young Stanley's now, see if he'll help me wrangle that devil on Friday. Come on, Sidekick. Get them dude shoes in the car and let's drive up the road."

I put my presents in the back seat with the groceries and climbed in. The Stanley place was only six or seven miles up the river. I sat in the back seat and flipped through the new books.

Grandpa pulled into the yard at the Stanley ranch. The house was close to the main road and the driveway was graveled so there was no problem with the mud. Grandpa got out of the car and walked up to the house. The screen door opened and out came Charles Stanley. He was a short man, a little on the heavy side. He wore thick glasses and a straw hat.

He and Grandpa exchanged greetings and made the usual small talk about the weather and the crops that people around here always did. Finally, I heard Grandpa say, "On Friday I got a little job to do that requires two men, Charles. I wondered if you'd be available. There's a little money in it for you. I need to bring that three-year-old stallion down to the corral. The owner is coming to pick it up. I want to get it out of here. Can you do it?"

"I'd sure like to help you out, Henry, but Friday I got to leave with the truck to pick up some cattle from that Hereford breeder up near Hardin. I just got to pick up that stock on Friday. Why not get one of them Martin boys. They aren't much good, but . . . shucks, Henry, I remember watching you handle two or three broncs at a time all by yourself when you worked down at my dad's old ranch. Guess that was quite a few years ago though, huh?"

Grandpa looked down at his boots. He seemed embarrassed. "Well . . . you know what. My granddaughter here rode out to the pasture with me the other day. I think she could give me all the help I need out there on Friday. She'd sure be better than one of the Martin boys. They can't wrangle a milk cow out of a barn. Well, good to see you again, Charles. Stop by the house sometime soon."

Charles Stanley said something I couldn't hear and Grandpa came back to the car. I sat there stunned. Did Grandpa really think I could help him bring in that stallion?

When Grandpa got into the car, Grandma said, "Henry,

that is out of the question. You'll have to get one of the Martin boys. You can't take Janey with you to bring in that wild horse."

Grandpa's hands rested lightly on the steering wheel. He said in a strong voice: "Marie, I ain't foolish. I know Janey on a horse. I know what she can do. I trained her myself, didn't I? I've seen her and that old blue horse run steers for a mile—until they saw things her way. She's got guts—don't back off from a situation even if it makes her nervous."

Grandpa started the car and backed out of the yard. Grandma pressed her lips together tightly and stared out the front window without speaking. When we were back on the road Grandpa looked back at me and said, "What do you think, Janey? You want to ride with me on Friday?"

I sat there confused. Full of pleasure and fear. That Grandpa considered me equal to the job was the highest compliment he had ever paid me. But trailing a stallion gone wild was scary. I remembered the way the horse looked as he pawed the mud and snorted at Grandpa and Smoky last week. I didn't know what to say. I looked down, trying to decide. There in my lap was my new book, *Thunderhead*. The picture on the jacket was of a magnificent white horse running, wild and fierce, over the prairie with a dark and stormy sky in the background.

I knew I had to try.

Getting Ready

The sunlight came through my bedroom window and then disappeared again as a cloud passed over it. I could hear Grandma downstairs in the kitchen. The chickens had already been let out and were clucking and scratching by the porch below. I rubbed my eyes. Then I remembered—it was Friday. Already! I had to get up.

I jumped out of bed and dressed. My long, skinny legs seemed more unruly than usual as I hurriedly pulled on my dungarees. When I buttoned up I felt my stomach jump as though it were overrun with grasshoppers. I grabbed my old boots and headed through the hallway and down the stairs. I didn't want Grandpa to have to call me. Not today.

In the kitchen Grandma was taking the frying pan of bacon off the top of the stove.

"Morning, Grandma. Is Grandpa still here?"

"You know he is. He was up before it was light. The dogs were fussing and he thought it might be a chicken-stealing skunk, but he didn't find anything. Right now he's up at the barn saddling the horses." She went to the pantry and came back with some eggs.

The grasshoppers started acting up in my stomach again.

Grandma continued, "You know I don't approve of this.

Henry has had you out seeing and doing things no young girl should. Last winter when he had you play vet's assistant to that cow's breech birth I was angry, and then you found the dead calf last week. Now this stallion. Your folks wouldn't approve. I told Henry so, but he won't listen."

As Grandma spoke she was breaking eggs into the pan and hurling the shells into the garbage pail. Her back was turned toward me. Several strands of her long gray hair escaped the bun at the nape of her neck and dangled on the collar of her flowered shirt. Grandma didn't wear dungarees like the rest of us. She wore slacks or even dresses.

"Your father has the right idea, Janey. Those trips he makes you take to Minneapolis every year are good for you. You *should* be exposed to something besides just cowboying. I'm going to start you sewing this summer, too. We can get you ready for your trip."

I heard Grandpa talking to the dogs as he crossed the porch. The screen door slammed and he walked through the washroom and into the kitchen. He tossed his hat on a chair. His bald head was already sunburned. "Morning, Janey. I got the horses saddled. You ready?"

"Yeah. I guess so," I said softly.

" 'Guess so'? You better know so, Sidekick. That big red fella will put a hoof right through a guess." He chuckled and turned toward Grandma. "Breakfast ready, Marie? Just answer yes or no. No 'guess so's,' " he chuckled again.

Grandma was irritated. She had her lips pressed together tightly when she brought the bacon and scrambled eggs to the table. She nearly forgot the French toast she had been keeping warm in the oven.

We sat down at the table. Grandpa said to me, "Now don't pick at your breakfast. Eat up. We're not bringing any lunch because this ain't no picnic. I expect we will be up in the upper pasture by ten. May have to spend some time finding the horse, unless he obliges us by charging like he did last time. One of those mares is due to foal—I hope she hasn't already. That might make him tougher. Anyway, as soon as we find him, we've got to split him from the mares. That'll take some time, too. We should have him on the way back to the river by noon. And sure as the sage smells, there won't be any stopping or resting once we start pushing him. If we do our job, riding close, and not backing down, we should see the corral by three or four o'clock." Grandpa had been eating and talking between bites. He paused and looked at me. "So like I said, eat up!"

I couldn't swallow. I had been chewing the same bite of bacon throughout his speech. Now I tried some eggs, because he was staring at my plate. The grasshoppers in my stomach were turning into frogs. I smiled at Grandpa and took another bite of eggs, even though I hadn't swallowed the first.

He nodded approval. "That's more like it." His plate was empty. He pushed his chair away from the table. "I'm going up to the barn and check on Polly. You finish your breakfast and come along."

As soon as we heard him leave the porch, Grandma said, "Now you take your time. He's going to go up there and lean on the corral fence and roll a cigarette. You've got time."

Grandma knew I was nervous. She wouldn't talk about it, but she knew. I wondered if she had ever been nervous or scared. She could do everything from killing snakes to holding a calf for branding, but she did it as though she were a visitor on the ranch participating in an adventure. Grandma and her family had come to Montana as homesteaders over fifty years ago, but she still acted sort of like her life here was temporary, that soon she'd be going back to her lovely house on Lake Superior outside of Duluth, Minnesota. Grandma had an air. She would kill a chicken, clean it, cook it and then serve it at the dining-room table as though it had been done for her by a servant. She never complained, but you could tell when she didn't like something. She'd always tried to keep me out of the rough side of ranch life, but if I chose to go there, she didn't expect me to complain either.

She was heating water for dishes on the stove and bringing out the flour, yeast and milk for making bread. I couldn't finish my breakfast. I finally pushed my plate away. Grandma picked up the remains and took it to the pan for the dogs. She didn't say a word about waste.

"Get your hat. It might clear today, and the sun will be hot," she cautioned. I went to the washroom and picked out my old straw hat with the tie under the chin, then I went back to the kitchen to tell her I was leaving.

She took her hands out of the dough she was mixing, wiped them on her apron and gave me a big hug. "You do a good job, now. You are a capable and brave girl. I know you can do it."

With that Grandma squeezed me closer. I felt little and comforted. I was afraid I would start to cry. Grandma understood. She released me just in time. I kissed her cheek and turned, ran out through the washroom and jumped the two porch steps, landing evenly on both boots, and started for the barn.

Grandpa had tied the horses to the hitching rail in front of the barn. He was working on a piece of rope as I approached.

"I'm almost done with yours, Janey," he said as he gave

a test yank to the big monkey's fist he had tied to the end of a piece of lariat.

"Here, try this bola. We better test it for length before we start. I don't want it too long for you to handle."

I took the rope. "Let me see you get that swinging," he said. "Get that ball on the end going in a big circle."

I tried, but it was heavy and I couldn't keep it going. The knot fell to the ground.

"Give it back to me," Grandpa ordered. "I've got to cut off at least a foot."

He took out his knife and lopped off a piece of the rope and gave the bola back to me. I could turn it now and keep it spinning.

"Good." Grandpa nodded. "Listen, Sidekick, when we are pushing that red horse and he gets mean about it and runs at you and Blue, I want you to get that rope going. I mean spinning fast with that knot whipping the air like a willow in a cyclone. That'll keep Big Red at a polite distance. He's liable to try to get a taste of Blue or scare both of you with some fancy hoof work, but if you've got that bola flying and he gets a nip of it, he'll learn to keep his distance. You understand? Anytime I see the horse coming your way, I don't want to see that rope hanging loose. Do you hear me?"

I nodded. I tried to get the bola going again. It was hard work and it made my arms hurt. I wondered how much of this I would have to do. I began to have second thoughts. Grandma was right, I shouldn't be riding with Grandpa today. I didn't really need to know how to corral wild horses. It was too much. It was dangerous. I couldn't do it.

"Well, Janey, let's get started. We're going to have a cool ride to the upper pasture. I think we'll cross the river at the water gap below the alfalfa. See if it's going to be ready for cutting soon. Might even see a baby antelope or two. I saw a couple of pronghorn does up there looking about ready a while back."

He untied the reins, mounted Smoky and looked at me expectantly. I started to say, "I don't want . . ." but stopped mid-sentence.

"What? Speak up?"

I said, "I don't want the dogs to follow us. We'd better have Grandma put them in the house until we're gone."

"You're right. We'll ride by the house and tell her."

I climbed up on Blue and followed Grandpa down to the house. Grandpa yelled for Grandma to get the dogs. She opened the screen and called them. When they didn't come, she came out and picked up Heinie and tucked him under her arm. She grabbed Pal's collar with her free hand and coaxed him toward the house. He didn't want to go with her. He hated to miss an outing. For a minute, I wished I could stay home with Pal.

Grandma called to me through the screen door. "You remember what I said. Do a good job and take care, Janey."

I just sat there looking back at her. Finally I jerked Blue's reins and nudged him with my boot heel. We started down the hill toward the river.

Grandpa rode ahead of me. The sun was behind the clouds again, so the prairie was shaded and cool. We crossed the alfalfa bottom at an easy trot. The alfalfa was blooming and the blossoms were covering the plants like tiny purple feather dusters. The smell of it was a perfume I'd admired all my life. I loved it from the time it blossomed until it had been mown and was lying on the ground ripening into the winter's hay. It smelled like food. Once, when I was about four, I tried to eat alfalfa hay out of the milk cow's feed bin.

I remember my mother yelling as she saw me standing there chewing away on a big mouthful of hay. I smiled to myself. Blue dipped his head, hoping to grab a bit of that sweetness on the run. I gave him a little slack on the rein so he could have a nibble, and hoped Grandpa wouldn't turn around. He didn't approve at all—said it developed a bad habit.

We were at the edge of the field already, nearing the river. Here the alfalfa gave way to the heavier smell of the willow blossoms. The willows grew in the damp area close to the river. There was the thickness of the river mud in their smell.

Grandpa slowed to a walk and turned to me. "River's down. I don't think they'll be swimming, but we'd better let them pick their own way."

With that he headed Smoky down the mud bank. I pulled Blue up to give Grandpa time to get a head start in the water. I wanted to see if he had to swim. I didn't mind the idea so much this time, but I liked to know beforehand if it was going to happen.

The water was over Smoky's knees about a quarter of the way across. I started down the bank and into the water. The current was curling around the lower portion of Smoky's haunches, but he was halfway now. Unless he hit a hole, he wouldn't have to swim. The very moment I thought that, Smoky's behind dropped down into the water. His tail was floating. I saw Grandpa jerk his feet out of the water and wrap them around the saddle horn. Smoky was swimming hard through the current toward the other side. Then it was my turn. Blue had seen Smoky's path, and he was ready. I could feel him push off the edge of the sand bar. I had my feet up already. I wasn't going to get wet. Smoky was scrambling up the steep bank in powerful pulling leaps as Blue's feet hit the gravel river bed again. When we pulled up on the bank, Grandpa was sitting there with his wet boots dripping from his stirrups.

"Did you get wet?" he asked.

"Nope. I saw where you went in and pulled my feet up just in time," I answered smugly.

Grandpa grinned and pulled his reins to the left. Smoky responded and off we went, walking now, to give the horses a breather. The prairie gumbo was already drying, forming deep cracks. The gumbo was like that. One day it was the slickest, stickiest mud you ever saw, and the next it looked like the face of a wrinkled old man.

A few saucy prairie dogs popped out of their holes and scolded us as we rode by. I saw a gray cottontail bound out of the dark green of a greasewood bush. A meadowlark sang across the prairie. Occasionally, there was the *scree* of a hawk, but it wasn't one of those noisy days when the crickets are complaining and the grasshoppers are flying around like B-42's. The prairie was peaceful and I felt happy and calm. My nervousness was gone.

Grandpa turned to me and pointed toward the bluff which sat back about a quarter of a mile from the river. Following his finger, I couldn't see anything at first, but as my eyes adjusted to the distance, two spots of tan just slightly darker than the gumbo appeared. It was a pronghorn antelope doe and her young one. I couldn't see the baby as clearly from that distance. The doe was staring hard at us through her dark mask. She was beautiful. I wanted to ride over and get a closer look at the baby, but knew this wasn't the time. I thought about the high jump. School was so far away.

Seeing the baby antelope made me wonder if we'd find a colt up in the pasture. Maybe they would let me have it. I'd been begging for a horse of my own ever since I'd learned to ride, but Daddy said it was silly—we already had enough horses and since I was only on the ranch on holidays and in the summer, I'd have to be content with big slow Blue.

We were at the gate for the upper pasture. Grandpa dismounted to open it and led Smoky through. I followed and waited while he mounted up. He left the gate open.

"Judging by the condition of the gumbo, I figure they'll be up by the back reservoir. They'll want to stay close to water at foaling time," Grandpa said.

"Grandpa?" I ventured.

"Yup."

"Have you ever done this before? I mean have you driven a stallion away from his mares before?"

"You know now, it's funny, but I don't think I have. I've wrangled for forty-odd years, too. Maybe I just can't remember. Anyway, I'm sure I can figure out how to do it even if I don't have any—what's that the hands say now when they are looking for work—previous experience. You worried that when that stallion runs at us I'll sit there and leave it all up to you? Come to think of it, that's not a bad idea. You and Blue take care of the red fella and I'll come in only if you call me."

I smiled. At least he was feeling good, and that made me feel better.

Grandpa pulled his Bull Durham sack out of his shirt pocket, wrapped his reins around the horn and rolled a cigarette as we rode. "Janey," he said. "I know you are, ah, excited. Just remember two things. The stallion is wild now. As far as he's concerned, we're trespassing, threatening his women. He is a natural animal. He doesn't know we're doing

it for his own good and he doesn't care if he gets a dozen mares when he leaves this ranch. He has his life here and he will fight like mad to keep it. That's one. Now two, just keep that bola going. I'm not asking you to do anything you can't do. Just remember what I said and stay awake. You're going to see a trick or two today."

We rode along in silence after that.

"There they are, Janey," Grandpa said.

I looked over the sage and greasewood. There were four horses on the side of a hill. Three were grazing, but one was standing at attention, watching us.

Flying Hooves

"That's him. We'll ride over and see what his first move's going to be. The sooner we separate him from the mares, the better. Here he comes," Grandpa said softly.

The stallion was trotting in our direction. His head was high, his gold mane catching the breeze. He stopped, looked back at the mares and whinnied, then came on toward us.

At a distance there was nothing alarming about him. He was beautiful. The sun was weaving in and out among the clouds. It made light and shadow jigsaw pieces of the prairie. The stallion passed through a patch of light. His hide shone like the stone of a carnelian ring I'd seen in a jewelry store window in Minneapolis. We walked toward him, he trotted toward us. The distance between was closing rapidly. Grandpa stopped. He motioned for me to do the same.

"Let him come to us now. We'll be that much closer to the gate. The mares are staying back. Good. When he tries to push us out, let him. Move toward the gate. Let him take us through the gate instead of us taking him. Maybe we can bait him all the way back to the barn." Grandpa smiled. His eyes had not left the stallion as he spoke.

The stallion was close. I could see the dust puffs as his hooves hit the gumbo. He looked all perky and curious.

Suddenly, as if he recognized an old foe, he put his head down, ears back, and galloped straight at Smoky. I watched as the stallion ran right up, practically on top of Grandpa, then stopped so quickly his weight was thrown onto his powerful back haunches. His front feet were off the ground, climbing the air. That's how it looked, as if they were climbing stairs of air. It must have happened quickly, but I saw it in slow-motion. The stallion seemed to be up on his hind legs forever. He gave a long, high-pitched whinny. Then his front feet descended. They floated down. His mane flew out about his head and neck in a red-gold flame. He pivoted on his haunches and bared his teeth, then turned toward me. My mind went blank. There was no time. The horse neared Blue's shoulder. His eyes were big and glowing. His ears were back, hardly visible in his mane, his mouth open, his teeth huge. I yanked Blue's reins to the right and kicked him hard. Blue didn't need the kick. He saw those teeth coming for his shoulder and turned like a ball bearing. The stallion slid by us.

I heard Grandpa yelling, "Head for the gate! Let him chase you!"

I didn't look to see what the stallion was doing. I took off for the gate. There was the pounding of hooves close behind me. The bola! I reached down and tried to untie the saddle strings, but I was moving too fast and was shaking. Twice, the strings slipped from my fingers. No use. The stallion was closing in. He was cutting close to me. I sensed his head near my leg, and reined to the right. Blue was no match in speed. Where was Grandpa? I didn't know what to do. We weren't heading for the gate anymore. Blue was running as hard as he could. The stallion was all around us. His mane brushed my legs. I didn't know where I was going. I was aware only of the horses' breathing and heaving as we careened through the sagebrush. Suddenly, Grandpa and Smoky were right in front of us. The stallion stopped short in surprise. He galloped off a ways and stood.

"Get that bola out and keep it out!" Grandpa ordered. "You're letting him get too close. He nearly had his teeth in your leg that time. If you'd had that rope turning, he wouldn't have come in and turned you. You gave him a taste of control. Now he'll think he's the kingpin." Then, without the slightest trace of sympathy, "Got shaken up right in the beginning, didn't you. That should show you that there's no dreaming time out here today. That stallion is about the toughest, smartest horse you're going to come upon. Damn pretty, too," he added.

I untied the saddle strings and clutched the bola. The stallion was standing, waiting. He tossed his mane and pawed the dirt with one hoof. Grandpa gave Smoky a kick and rode directly toward him. The big red horse went up on his hind legs again. He was fast. Flying feet reached through the space between him and Grandpa. Grandpa's bola was whirling above his head. As the stallion's front legs came down, the knot on the end connected. There was red confusion, mane and tail flaring, meeting. The stallion had pivoted and was now kicking both back legs at Smoky's chest. Grandpa jerked on the reins and Smoky wheeled just in time. He was only grazed on the shoulder. Grandpa let out a whoop. *"Whooee!"*

With bola flying he charged the stallion from the side. The stallion ran out in front of him.

"Move in, Janey. We're goin' for the gate!" Grandpa bellowed.

I gave Blue a hard kick. Grandpa was coming up on

Smoky. We had the stallion in a V-wedge between us. We ran toward the gate. Then, as if he got the picture, the stallion accelerated. Grandpa was whooping and spurring Smoky. He yelled at me to pick it up. When I tried to kick Blue, I realized I was shaking all over. Grandpa kept yelling and screaming at Smoky, the stallion and me.

The stallion turned on Smoky again. Grandpa let out a whole string of powerful cusses. His bola was going and he wasn't swinging in a protective circle. He was aiming this time. The stallion caught a fierce whap on the top of his head. He slowed for a moment, dazed, then shivered, one of those jelly shivers, where all the muscles move at once. Grandpa charged him, yelling and swearing.

"Get in here, you!" Grandpa moved my way. "Push him! Push him!"

The gate was closer. Grandpa yelled and spun his bola. He and Smoky were everywhere. He was five men on horseback. The stallion was confused. Grandpa was a whirlwind, spinning Smoky and *Hey-yah*-ing like an entire rodeo. The stallion was moving along in front of him. We were on top of the gate now. I wanted to get him out of this pasture, too. I began to yell and spin my bola so hard, my arm felt as though it would fly off. The stallion was looking from side to side as though he might try to break for it. There was the gate.

"Move! Move!" Grandpa stormed. It was all noise and motion. My legs grabbed the saddle as I swung my bola with one hand and reined with the other. The stallion turned toward me and reared. I could feel the air move as his hooves flew over my head.

The bola! Swing! Swing! Turn Blue. Turn him. The stallion came down, hooves thrashing, where Blue and I had been seconds before. Grandpa was right behind him. Whipping his bola, he swung at the horse. He hit his haunch and the stallion bolted forward. He was through the gate. We followed, both pushing with bolas flying. The stallion broke into a gal- lop and headed toward the bluff.

We let him go. Grandpa dismounted in a flash and ran for the gate. He dragged it closed and fastened it. Back on Smoky, he gave me a look. All he said was, "Let's go."

As he walked past me I saw the blood on Smoky's shoulder. "Grandpa! Stop! Smoky is bleeding," I shouted.

"Don't you think I know it. Old Red got a hunk. That's why I got serious with that bola," he said as we continued toward the bluff.

"The next thing we have to worry about is the cotton-woods—and the river bank where it drops off at the bend. He might try to pin us to a tree or shove us into the river. He's smart enough. I sure don't want to have to fish you and that fat horse you're riding out of the river. I think I'd just wait until you washed up on a sand bar," he laughed.

It wasn't funny to me. It was cruel. He got tougher and tougher. He must have known how frightened I was, but he wouldn't tolerate fear. It made him mad.

We were getting close to the stallion again, and he snorted a warning. I could see the sweat-darkened spots on his flanks. I reached down and ran my hand over Blue's shoulder. He was dripping wet. Smoky's shoulder was pink where the blood had mingled with sweat.

The stallion's eyes were flashing like caution lights. He tossed his mane and switched his tail as we closed in. I gripped the bola and started it twirling as I kept Blue steady ahead. Up reared the stallion, whinnying and striking at the air. As his feet landed he turned abruptly and broke into a fast gallop back toward the gate. Grandpa and Smoky raced after him. Grandpa was spurring Smoky ferociously and Smoky was running like a two-year-old colt. They were neck and neck with Red, but they had to get in front to turn him. Grandpa was riding low and way out over Smoky's neck. He had his bola going. I saw him reach out to the side with it. He kept whipping at the stallion. The stallion turned. Grandpa had turned him. They were both running full tilt toward the river crossing. I was doing my best to keep up and praying that the stallion would go right on running all the way to the corral. Please. Please.

The stallion slowed. Grandpa motioned for me to cut down quickly. We matched his pace. The stallion stopped. We walked slowly up behind him. He let fly with both hooves, a real mule kick. One hoof connected with Blue's chest. Blue stumbled and rolled toward one side, but regained his balance before he fell. The stallion turned and ran at Smoky with teeth ready. There was dust and the smell of trampled sagebrush. Grandpa was hollering. So was I. My bola was spinning, but I didn't know why. The red horse charged. I felt my bola connect with something. There was a fierce whinny. The stallion reared. Grandpa rode in on him from the side. He hit him hard on the ribs. The horse turned toward me again, ears back and teeth ready. He snapped his jaws. I felt a rein being jerked out of my hand. The rein fell to the ground below Blue's head. I leaned out to get it. The stallion ran at me. I kept spinning my bola. There was no word for my fear. The stallion backed away, but I couldn't reach the rein. Grandpa rode at the horse. The stallion whirled and charged him. I reached again for the rein and got it. I looked over. Grandpa and the stallion we sashaying like

partners in a square dance. I had a hysterical urge to giggle. Nothing seemed real.

Grandpa's voice cut through the dust. "Janey, don't just stand there."

I kicked Blue and moved toward the odd dance. The stallion leaped forward, all four legs stiff, then ran toward the river bank. Grandpa and Smoky were right behind, then me and Blue. The bank was steep on this side of the river, especially on the bend where the current had cut it away. It wasn't safe to ride a horse near the edge because it was only a gumbo shelf with the river running beneath. The stallion seemed to know. He slowed down about six feet from the edge and turned. He flew with fury at Grandpa, reared, landed, turned, kicked, spun and dived at Smoky with his teeth bared. Smoky leaped and whinnied. Grandpa cussed and screamed. He spurred Smoky headfirst into the stallion's ribs. He bellowed and beat at the big red horse with his bola. The horse ran toward the embankment, Grandpa and Smoky with him. They were too close. Grandpa drew Smoky up short. He almost sat him on his haunches. The stallion didn't stop. There was a weird sound, like a wire being stretched, as the bank gave way. Dust billowed everywhere. I saw the stallion's mane and tail floating upward, shrouded in a gray mist, then heard a splash.

Grandpa was off Smoky, running to the edge. I got down from Blue as fast as I could. Grandpa stood there, his mouth open in disbelief. I looked down. The stallion was halfway across the river, unhurt. He was running through the river. The water was belly-deep and still the stallion kept running.

"Come on! We've got to get over there," Grandpa shouted.

We mounted, went to the nearest crossing and rode

through the willows along the river's edge. Grandpa saw him first. He was galloping through the cottonwoods, heading back to the upper pasture. We caught up to him, but it wasn't easy. Our horses were tired. The stallion turned on us, but without the same fight. He backed away before he was within striking distance. We were able to turn him without much trouble. It was crazy. After all the fighting, there we were, heading through the pasture toward the corral, the stallion trotting in front of us.

I started to cry. There was no reason now, but I cried. I couldn't stop. The noise of the horses, trotting and huffing, muffled some of my sobs but Grandpa heard me anyway and looked over. The stallion was practically in the gate and I was bawling my eyes out.

"Shut up that hollering!" Grandpa snapped. "We've got to finish this thing."

The stallion went through the gate and into the corral. Grandpa was off Smoky and had the gate shut and fastened in two seconds. It was a big wooden corral. The stallion raced over to the opposite fence, almost crashed into it. He stopped as if surprised and spun around in that now-familiar way. He ran back toward the gate. He reared. He came down on the gate with his hooves, but the pine boards were heavy and it held. He turned and ran wildly around the corral, bucking, charging the fence. He ran in circles, tossing his mane, whinnying, kicking. I cried harder.

"Get out of here with that racket," Grandpa yelled. "We're done. Why are you blubbering now?"

I couldn't answer. I couldn't move. I could only cry. I felt Blue move. Grandpa had ridden up on Smoky and grabbed my reins. He led Blue around the corral toward the barn. I closed my eyes as tight as I could and bit my lips. Blue stopped. I felt hands around my waist and I was lifted from the saddle. My feet touched the ground.

"Get on down to the house," Grandpa ordered. "I've got to tend the horses. Got to look at those bites on Smoky."

My legs didn't know how to walk. I hated to open my eyes. A long cry, high and shaky, burst on my ears. It sounded like that sheep did the night the coyotes got him. I opened my eyes. The stallion had his nose tilted up into the air like a howling dog. I turned and ran toward the house without looking back.

Hurting

Grandma was in the kitchen. I ran through, into the hallway and up the stairs to my room. She called after me. I heard her in the hallway and I slammed the door to my room.

"Janey? Janey? Are you all right?"

I heard her on the stairs, then at my door. "Janey? Let me in. You sound terrible. Are you hurt?"

"No."

"Let me see you anyway. I baked some cinnamon rolls today and I've got the one with the most caramel on the bottom waiting for you in the warming oven." She opened the door.

I was sitting on the floor.

She bent down and scooped me into her arms. She didn't say a word. I pressed my face into her shoulder and wept. Grandma rocked me back and forth.

She took off my boots and my filthy dungarees, got a wet washcloth and wiped off my face and hands. Then she left, saying she would call me for supper.

When I woke it was dark. I moved my leg. It felt terribly stiff. I lay there thinking about the stallion, I thought of many things. The flying hooves, menacing teeth, the golden mane floating on the water when the horse fell through the river bank.

I could hear the river running now, in the quiet of the night. There was an owl hooting out by the sheep shed. The house was still. Grandma must have let me sleep through supper. I was so sore. I tried to identify the pains. My arms were stiff from swinging the bola and my legs throbbed from gripping the saddle so hard. My back ached all over. There was something more bothering me. What was it?

I remembered the time Grandpa had set a trap in front of the chicken coop to catch a raccoon that had stolen a chicken a night for four nights. In the morning we went to check the trap. It had been sprung by the marauder, but all we had caught of him was three toes. They were still in the trap. The raccoon had chewed them off and escaped. Grandpa took the dogs and trailed him. They found the raccoon hiding in a fallen tree down by the slough. He couldn't climb to the safety of a tree with his toes gone. The dogs dragged the raccoon out of the tree. He fought them bravely, hissing and biting. I was afraid they would be hurt, but they were more than equal to the injured raccoon. When I saw they were going to kill him, I begged Grandpa to call them off. He looked at me as though I were crazy and asked me if I wanted to turn the whole chicken coop over to the "coon." I wanted to scream "Yes!" but knew better. I ran back to the house. I could hear the raccoon crying out like a terrified baby at the end. I went into my closet with my hands over my ears. I crawled back into the triangle where the slanted roof and the floor met, and stayed there until I cried myself to sleep. I was six then. Now I was twelve, but I still didn't understand.

A coyote howled somewhere far out on the prairie. The

river whispered. Some frogs were singing in the slough. I listened to the night sounds and waited for sleep. The sky was turning light before it came.

The dogs were barking. Everyone was up. The sun blared in my window. It must be late. I started to climb out of bed and flopped back down. I was stiff everywhere. I had on the dirty shirt that I had worn all day yesterday. My mouth tasted of dust and tears.

Sounds filtered up the stairs from the kitchen. Grandpa. I pulled the quilt over my head.

Grandma called up the stairs, "Janey, breakfast is ready." I uncovered my head and said, "I'm coming."

It took forever to get dressed. I ached all over and just couldn't seem to get going this morning. Finally I started downstairs. Grandpa's voice met me.

"Here she is. Janey, this is Tim Gilmore. He and Jack Thompson, his hand, are going to load the stallion this morning and get him down to some new mares in Wyoming."

I said hello to Mr. Gilmore. He was a tall, heavy man dressed in a blue-flowered cowboy shirt and dungarees. His stomach hung over the top of his pants, almost covering a big silver belt buckle with a bucking horse stamped on it.

Grandpa continued, "I was just telling Tim about the time we had bringing that horse in. Just the two of us. Never saw a horse fight like that. No sir, never did. I'll tell you, Tim. If I'd had any other hand with me than Janey, here, you would be riding after that horse yourself this morning. A paid hand would have pulled out before the pasture gate or asked for a bonus. Matter of fact, I doubt I could pay anyone to do that job. You'll see what I'm talking about when you load him. He's got plenty of spunk left . . . even after yesterday."

I couldn't believe my ears. Grandpa was bragging about me! After all those mistakes I'd made—after crying like a baby. Suddenly my stomach grumbled. Everyone laughed.

Grandma came in from the pantry carrying a jar of fresh cream. "Janey, honey. Sit down. You must be starving. You haven't eaten a thing since your breakfast yesterday and I think the dogs ate most of that."

She piled my plate with pancakes. There was fresh butter and chokecherry syrup. I ate everything and drank two glasses of milk. Grandpa and Mr. Gilmore had a second cup of coffee and a cigarette. They talked about the price of cattle.

Finally, Grandpa stood up. "Let's get up to the corral and see what the big fella has in mind this morning. Janey, you come on up, too."

I wasn't sure I wanted to see the stallion again.

Grandma was heating dishwater. "Want me to heat some water for you to wash up, Janey? I expect you are pretty sore. Warm water always helps that. Too bad I can't heat you a whole tub, but I've got to use the stove for cooking. Your Uncle Ed is coming today and it looks like we'll have Mr. Gilmore and his hand at noon. Listen to me go on. I haven't even asked you how you were feeling."

"I'm okay now, Grandma. Grandma?" I asked.

"Yes, honey."

"Did Grandpa say anything about me? About my crying or anything?"

"Your Grandpa said you were a good hand, that you faced the stallion with courage and never gave him the upper hand."

I decided to go to the corral. I told Grandma I would wash up later and was out the door before she could protest.

The dogs were waiting for me. Heinie sensed my good mood. He bounced after me, nipping at my pant legs. We ran through a bunch of chickens scratching at some spilled grain, and they scattered and squawked in four directions.

Grandpa and Mr. Gilmore were examining the loading chute. A pickup truck with a stock rack had been backed up to the chute. They were getting ready to adjust the ramp to the back of the pickup.

Grandpa turned to me. "Hey, Janey! Glad you're here. Now we can have a smoke while you get that horse in the truck."

Grandpa was in a good mood. I guess he was relieved to be getting the stallion out of here. The dogs began to bark and ran toward the mailbox. Uncle Ed was driving up the road in his dark green truck.

Ed was mother's brother, Grandma and Grandpa's youngest son. He looked like Grandpa, thin and wiry. He worked in town as mechanic at the Caterpillar Tractor place, but he loved the ranch and came out often. He would saddle up a horse, usually Smoky, put a bedroll on the back, tie on his rifle and go out for a couple of days at a time. Sometimes he'd take Pal with him. Once when Pal had been off with Uncle Ed the dog was bitten by a rattlesnake. Ed cut the bite and drew out as much of the poison as he could. He carried Pal back to the house across the front of his saddle. Ed sat up all night nursing him. No one expected Pal to live, but in the morning he stood up and wobbled over to the horse trough for a drink of water. I owed Pal's life to Uncle Ed.

Ed drove right up to the corral. Grandpa introduced him to Mr. Gilmore. Uncle Ed asked, "Are you the Gilmore of the G-Bar-T Ranch, the spread that supplies the rodeo buckers?"

"Yes, I am. And according to Henry's description of this

stallion's tricks, I've got myself a good breeder. How did you know about my place?"

"You supplied over half the horses for the last buckin' horse sale down in town," Ed said. "They had a write-up in the paper. Talked about the special ways of training you had on your ranch to make those horses so mean. Your stock drew the highest prices from the rodeo buyers because they were such wicked buckers." There was a sharp edge to Ed's voice. I didn't like what I'd heard at all.

Mr. Gilmore acknowledged Ed's information with a nod. Grandpa asked him if he had bought the big red horse as a colt, intending to raise him as a bucker.

"Oh, no, Henry! I bought him because he was the colt of that mean ol' Sunfish that traveled with the Wylie Brothers' Rodeo for years. One of the wildest horses ever ridden in a ring. I always intended to use this horse for stud purposes. From what you've been telling me, seems like I made a good decision," Mr. Gilmore said.

Ed turned to Grandpa. "What happened with the horse? What have you been telling him?"

Grandpa gave him a short description of the drive the day before, adding that I had done a "whale of a job."

Ed grinned at me, "Earning your keep this summer, huh? It's about time." He turned back to Grandpa. "If there is a job to do, let's get it over with so I can ride over to the south forty, do the fencing and get some target practice in before dark."

They went into the barn and returned a few minutes later carrying lariats and a loading whip. Grandpa and Ed decided they would go into the corral and push the horse into the chute. Mr. Gilmore and his hired hand would close the chute gate and move him through the chute into the truck.

Grandpa and Ed entered the corral. They walked toward the stallion, their lariats ready. I knew they didn't plan to rope the horse, but they would spin them to get him moving or to keep him away from them, as Grandpa and I had used bolas. The stallion watched them warily.

There was a loud squeak as the chute gate was raised on its pulleys, leaving an opening from the corral into the chute. The stallion turned toward the noise. He was facing the gate. Mr. Gilmore and his hired hand jumped back out of sight after they raised the gate. The stallion sniffed at the opening in the fence. He moved cautiously in that direction. We were quiet, hoping he would walk into the chute on his own, thinking it was a way out of the corral. The horse tossed his mane. The sunlight danced across the white streak on his forehead. He snorted and took another step toward the chute, then another. Another. His head was in the chute. Another. Another. He stopped. We waited. Grandpa could have hurried him in, I knew, but he wanted him calm. I squeezed the corral post and wished the stallion into the chute with all my strength. The horse took a step back, then another. He stopped. His backside was still sticking out of the chute. They couldn't drop the gate yet. Grandpa spun his lariat over his head and threw it. It hit the stallion's rump with a whap. The horse jumped. He was in. Mr. Gilmore released the pulley ropes and the chute gate dropped behind him.

In seconds, those familiar front hooves rose high up over the sides of the chute. A fierce whinny, then a crash as the back hooves kicked into the chute gate. The stallion kicked and bucked as the men urged him forward with the loading whip. The horse tried to turn. He couldn't. The chute was too narrow. He could only move forward or break the chute. The men were all yelling and cussing.

Ed jumped up on the side of the chute, lariat turning. He roped the horse. He tried to pull him up the ramp. It seemed to be working. Then the stallion reared. The rope was stripped from my uncle's hands. The stallion paused in mid-air. In the craziness of the moment I thought he might fly away like the flying red horse I'd seen in the night sky over Minneapolis, advertising gasoline. The stallion seemed to float in the air, then he went over. There was a loud, dead thump as he landed on his back in the chute. I heard Grandpa swearing. I ran to the chute. Four red legs thrashing around like tumbleweeds in a high wind. He was alive, but was lying on his back, and his mouth was frothing. His eyes had white showing all the way around. "Dear God," I prayed silently, "don't let him die like this."

Grandpa ordered the chute gate pulled up. The rope was still around the stallion's neck. Grandpa said they would have to drag him out of the chute. There was no room to turn him over. He headed for the barn to get a horse harnessed to pull the stallion out.

Mr. Gilmore was walking around fussing about losing a good breeder if the horse was hurt. I was furious. This whole thing was Mr. Gilmore's fault. The horse should have been trained, not left wild. Maybe Mr. Gilmore wanted him like this, so unmanageable. I became more and more angry—angry for yesterday, angry for the beautiful horse lying on his back, his eyes rolling in terror. Mr. Gilmore's voice fussed on. I was ready to scream at him when Ed interrupted.

"Just be quiet and give me a hand," he said. "We can untangle this rope so it will be ready when Henry gets back."

They went to work freeing the rope. Grandpa came out of the barn leading Blue. Blue could pull and he had already proved to be calm around the stallion. Ed was close to the stallion's head, trying to maneuver the rope into a good position for pulling. I wanted to leave, but couldn't move. Grandpa fastened the rope to Blue's harness.

"Watch that rope, now," he cautioned. "It's going to get tight. I don't know if we can do this without choking him."

Grandpa gave Blue the signal to pull. The rope tightened. There was movement in the chute. The stallion was struggling as the rope tightened about his neck. Blue stopped. Ed adjusted the rope. Blue pulled again. The stallion inched forward. Ed fixed the rope again. They pulled again and again. He was moving forward painfully, slowly. I felt as though he were being stretched. The stallion was still. I thought he must be dying. Dark things flew before my eyes. For a moment I thought I was seeing barn bats flying in the daytime. I became dizzy. My legs lost sensation. I hung onto the corral fence. It got dark. I gripped the fence tightly. The light slowly returned. The stallion was out of the chute.

Ed said, "That's good. He can make it now. Just take Blue out of here and we'll see if the stallion's all right."

They untied the rope. The stallion was lying on his back. He didn't seem to know or care that he was out of the chute and could stand. We waited. After a minute, which seemed like hours, he lifted his head and rolled to his side. He stayed there. Finally, he pulled his front legs under him and pushed himself up. He could stand. He hadn't broken his legs or back or anything. I wanted to shout so loud it would bounce off the big bluff across the river and come back to me.

Mr. Gilmore spoke first, "Well, I'll be . . . not a scratch. Let's load him up now, while he's still shaking. Isn't that something, though. Not a thing wrong with him after all that. *Whooee!* He is gonna be some stud. Let's get him in that truck."

Grandpa silently stared at him. Mr. Gilmore quieted down, then Grandpa spoke.

"Go right ahead, Tim. It's my guess that he'd do the same thing all over again, and I don't want any part of it. That horse would rather leave this place dead than leave it at all. I think you can forget loading him this weekend. I suggest that we stick him in the barn for a few days with nothin' to eat, turn him out Monday night or Tuesday morning with a chain around his neck so he can't go far, at least not across the river. Let him cool down a little, see what I mean? You drive back up here next weekend. We'll load him up nice and easy then. You load him like this, and even if you can get him in the pickup, he'll tip over before you get to the mailbox. You do what you want, but I'm through with this for the day. I'm going down to the house to eat."

With that, Grandpa walked off. I could tell he was disgusted with Mr. Gilmore, too. But I didn't like what Grandpa had said about locking the stallion in the barn and turning him out with a chain around his neck. I wondered what kind of chain he was talking about, but I knew better than to ask him now.

Everyone followed Grandpa to the house. Grandma had the table set and was frying chicken. Grandpa went out to the horse trough and brought back four bottles of beer. We used the horse trough to keep things cold when we ran out of ice for the ice box. The trough was constantly filled with artesian water which flowed from deep below the earth. Grandpa handed each of the men a beer. Grandma frowned.

The men sat down at the table with their beer. Grandpa took a swallow of beer. "I meant what I said up by the corral, Tim. I'm finished messing with that horse. He needs some breaking down before I'll do another thing with him. Go ahead and try to load him if you want, but I'll hold you responsible for anything he breaks, the chute or the corral, and Ed and I won't be there to help. Ed came out to do some fencing with me in the south forty, and that's what we're going to do as soon as we eat. You and Jack, here, are on your own. If you want to do like I said and come back next week, that's fine. Let me know what you decide."

When Grandpa finished the subject was closed. Mr. Gilmore might as well not be at the table. I knew Grandpa would ignore him until he left. I could see Ed grinning into his beer. He knew Grandpa, too. Mr. Gilmore sat there, knowing he had been dismissed.

Finally, he said, "I'll be back next Saturday morning. It's a long drive, but . . . ," he trailed off. Grandpa had put down his beer and was staring at him.

Grandma brought the dinner of fried chicken, biscuits and gravy. By each plate was a glass of fresh green onions in cold water. Grandpa loved to eat these with salt. He would put a pile of salt on the edge of his plate and dip the onion in and take a bite and dip it in again. I tried that, but it burned my mouth.

When lunch was over, Mr. Gilmore and his hired hand, Jack, thanked Grandma and complimented her. They said good-by. Grandpa waited until they drove off, then he went up to the barn with Ed to hitch up the team to the wagon, which was already loaded with the supplies he needed to fix the fence.

I helped Grandma clean up. Maybe I'd go down to the river this afternoon and catch some baby toads. I could take some soap and wash myself. It was pretty warm. I dried the dishes and stared out the window. I saw Ed up by the barn. He was leading the stallion from the corral with the rope. Grandpa was holding the horse-barn door open. Ed led the horse into the barn. I could no longer see them, but I imagined the stallion being tied in a stall. Grandpa and Ed came out and closed both the top and bottom of the split barn door.

The barn would be dark. I knew that the only light in there was what filtered in through the chinks between the boards. The mice ran around up in the loft making swishing tiptoe noises. The stallion only knew the open prairie and light. Grandpa was doing this to keep him from hurting himself, but . . . there didn't seem to be any good way to handle the stallion. My thoughts got muddled.

Grandma interrupted my thinking, "Janey, come in here for a minute." She was sitting in the big maroon velvet armchair in the living room. "What are you going to do this afternoon?" she asked.

"I thought I would go to the river and take a bath," I said.

"I thought you might like to go down to Mrs. Stanton's with me. I could take her some chokecherry syrup and you could play the piano."

Mrs. Stanton was an old widow who lived in a log house just down the river. She had a piano and a nice cool front porch. She and Grandma would sit on the front porch and talk while I pounded away on the piano in the parlor. It was fun, but I didn't want to go today.

"I don't really want to, Grandma," I answered. "I'm awfully stiff and I don't want to walk that far."

"Good enough. I thought it would get your mind off things. This stallion business has been too much for you, and to think it isn't over yet. I wish Henry hadn't been so stubborn with Mr. Gilmore. They probably could have loaded him this afternoon. The fencing could have waited until tomorrow."

"Grandma," I said. "You didn't see what happened this

morning. The horse got so wild when they put him in the chute that he almost killed himself."

Grandma sighed, "You shouldn't be involved in all that, Janey."

"I'm going down by the river now," I said abruptly, hoping that I didn't sound rude. I wanted to go bury my feet in the smooth mud and not talk or think about anything for a while. I ran through the washroom, grabbed a towel and headed for the river. The dogs had gone with Grandpa and Uncle Ed. Too bad. They would have been good company today.

On the way to the river I stopped at the slough. It was a full-fledged pond now, not just a boggy area. I found an old log to stand on at the water's edge. Looking for pollywogs was a good spring game. You had to sit quietly and stare into the muddy water until your eyes could see all the shades of the pollywogs as they scurried around down there, waiting to become frogs. The water was very thick today. The water spiders, which usually skimmed gracefully over the top of the water like skaters on ice, now seemed to be standing on top of chocolate pudding. I squatted on the log for a long time. My leg hurt, and I was about to give up when I saw one. Shiny, round and dark, like a wet pebble with a tail. It rose to the surface and returned to the darkness. More came.

When I tired of watching I went to the river. I bathed where the bottom was covered with red-pink shale so I wouldn't get muddy. I stretched my towel out in a sandy place and lay down to dry in the sun. A woodpecker was rat-a-tatting on a tree. I pretended he was tapping a rhythm for the humming of the river to follow. A breeze came up and the rustle of the cottonwoods and willows joined the afternoon sounds. I dozed off.

I woke from a dream of skating on the winter river. It was frozen but the ice was clear, and as I skated I could see the summer creatures, the catfish and minnows, the frogs and turtles, swimming and playing in the water beneath me. It was a good dream. I felt better, but it had grown cool. I gathered up my clothes, dressed quickly and ran up the hill to the house.

The Contraption

Grandpa and Ed had returned from fencing. The wagon stood by the barn, both doors to the horse barn were still closed.

Grandma was taking a big bowl of macaroni, tomatoes and hamburger out of the oven when I entered the kitchen. She said, "That was a long bath. I was about to send the dogs after you."

Grandpa and Ed came in from the grainery. We all sat at the table and talked about the fence in the south forty, the size of the hawk they had seen on their way out there. Not one word was said about the stallion.

While Grandma and I washed up, Ed went up to do the milking and Grandpa got out the gas lantern to fill it and put in a new mantle for the evening. Grandma reminded me to gather the eggs.

I took a pail and headed for the chicken coop. It was getting dark. The chickens were on the perches, shifting from side to side, getting comfortable and making clucking-cooing noises.

The middle row had six eggs, each in a different nest. Now I had to do the top row. I carefully reached in the first nest and felt around. No eggs. The second, one egg. The third, two eggs. The fourth, I changed to my left hand as my right arm was a little tired from reaching up. My hand moved around the straw, one, two and *ai-ee!* My hand closed around something cold with no ends, no limits like an egg. It squirmed in my grasp. I dropped my bucket and ran from the chicken house, screaming, "Grandpa, Grandpa, Pal . . . Come . . . Come . . . Grand . . !"

Grandma arrived first. I tried to tell her, but I got all mixed up. "Top row! Something in the nest! Eggs!"

She made me stop and take a breath, then tell her. Without saying a word she grabbed the rake which rested against the coop. She rushed into the coop. I was frightened, but also very curious, so I followed.

She turned to me. "Which nest, Janey?"

I pointed.

Grandma stood back and poked the rake handle into the nest. She moved it in slow circles, stirring the straw inside so it popped out the front hole. "He's still in there," she stated calmly.

"What's in there, Grandma?" I asked, amazed at her lack of fear.

"An egg-sucking bullsnake, that's what. He probably gets more mice from the granary than eggs from the chicken coop and he won't hurt us, so I don't want to hurt him, but he's not the nicest thing to put your hands on," she said. "I'm going to get him to twine around the rake handle, take him out of the nest, then give him to you to carry far enough away from here so he won't be able to find his way back."

I couldn't tell if she meant it or not, but I knew I didn't want to carry a bullsnake around the prairie on a rake handle in the dark.

I said, "Grandma, I think he might be too heavy for me and I'd have to drop him too near the coop."

She laughed, "Janey, that was as good a way to say 'Not on your life' as I've heard. But after that stallion you shouldn't let a bullsnake shake you up. That doesn't make any sense."

As she spoke, she manipulated the rake handle in the nest. "I think I've got him. You move out of my way. I'm going for the door fast."

Outside the coop I could see the snake clearly. It was big, about eighteen inches long, and as thick as the handle was. Its mouth was open and its tongue darted in and out. Grandma put the rake down by the gate. We stood back and watched as the bullsnake unwrapped itself and slid off in the dust of the cattle path.

Grandma put her arm around my shoulder and said, "This has been some day. Let's go back and get whatever eggs old Mr. Bullsnake left, and close up the coop before something less desirable than him gets in."

When the chores were done at last, Grandma sat down by the lamp to read. Grandpa went out on the back porch. I followed him. He sat on the second step, leaned back on the first and looked out at the moon rising over the hill.

We sat in silence for some time.

"Grandpa?" I ventured.

"Yep," he answered, still staring off into the darkness.

I paused, trying to decide how to say it, then plunged ahead. "Are you really going to put a chain around the stallion's neck?"

"Yep. The biggest log chain I can find, and I think I'll tie a log to it, too. We'll see how far he gets. Gotta do something," he said without looking at me.

I was too shocked to say anything at first. Finally I asked why.

The river gurgled below the hill. A mosquito buzzed near my ear. The moon rose over the rise at the end of the horse pasture, a sliver of silver like a shiny fingertip.

Grandpa didn't answer me right away. Then he sighed. "He don't know his place the way he is. He don't *have* a place the way he is. He's got to learn his place."

I was angry. I remembered my second-grade teacher once told me to stand in the hall until I "knew my place." I'd argued with her about how to spell "color." I'd said it was okay to spell it "colour" because I'd seen it that way in some of my father's books. Daddy explained later that they were British books, but it didn't change anything.

Besides, what about Grandpa? Who had ever put him in his place? Grandpa had run away from schools in St. Louis a total of seven times. When he was fifteen he made it all the way to Montana. His family found out where he was but they just let him go. He punched cattle on big ranches and then he met Grandma and they got married and started home-steading. Daddy said Grandpa never was any good at farm-ing. He knew horses and cattle, but not crops. He failed as a farmer. He couldn't keep a job. And I knew Grandpa had a reputation for drinking and gambling. Once I'd heard my uncles talking very secretly about bootlegging. I'd never paid much attention to what they said about Grandpa before, but now I thought about it. I wanted to say, "Who taught you your place?" but I couldn't talk to Grandpa that way. I was afraid I'd say something if I stayed there so I stood up. "I'm going to bed," I muttered.

"Good night," Grandpa replied, and went on staring off into the night.

I kissed Grandma and went up to my room. I undressed in the dark, took a blanket from my bed and climbed out the window onto the roof of the porch. I wasn't supposed to do this. There was a slope to the roof and Grandma was afraid I'd fall asleep and roll off. I wasn't worried. One afternoon, when no one was home, I'd gone out and hammered two boards into the roof to brace my feet against and to keep me from sliding. Now I could lie there and watch the stars twinkle and flash in the night. I could hear the river and feel the breeze without slipping at all. I was afraid to tell anyone, though, because right after I nailed down the boards, the porch roof began leaking.

I heard some coyotes calling to each other in the distance. The sound was beautiful, but lonely. I wondered why that was. Maybe because of the way the sound drifted for miles, reminding you how big the prairie was. Big and open. Then I thought of the stallion locked in the barn. I closed my eyes to block the image of the big red horse standing tied in a small stall in the dark barn. I opened my eyes and counted stars until I fell asleep.

I awoke in the middle of the night feeling cold and stiff, so I climbed back through the window and into my bed.

Getting up was much easier than it had been yesterday. I wasn't nearly so stiff. I hoped I would be able to ride with Uncle Ed today. That meant I had to talk to him right away. I dressed and ran downstairs.

No one was in the kitchen. I dashed out to the back porch. The three of them, Grandma, Grandpa and Ed, were up by the barn. I ran up there. They were talking and examining the side of the horse barn. I could see the boards of the barn, splintered and broken, jutting out in several places as though they had been chopped with an axe from the inside.

Ed said, "It's a cinch we've got to get him out of there. He'll bust down the whole place. Besides, Dad, we'd better get that chain on him while I'm still here to help you."

"You're right. The sooner we turn him out, the better. It's dangerous to keep him here. I'll be, though . . . Who'd have ever thought after yesterday . . . ," Grandpa's voice trailed off. He turned. "I'm going over to the machine shed to look for a chain. Why don't you get over to the woodpile, Marie, and get me a piece of log. Take the axe and groove it in the middle so I've got something to wrap the chain around."

"You come with me, Janey," Grandma said.

I followed her to the woodpile. She chose a piece of wood and we grooved in the middle just as Grandpa had said. I couldn't quite believe that this had anything to do with the stallion. I knew it did, but I didn't believe it. It was as if I were dreaming. Everything was blurry.

We got back to the barn as Grandpa walked up, carrying a piece of chain they had used to haul the cottonwood tree off the road after it was struck by lightning. It was about four feet long and had a big snap lock at one end. Grandpa took the piece of pine log and attached it securely to the chain with a piece of baling wire.

"You ready, Ed?" he asked.

"No, but I never will be for this job," Ed replied, heading for the horse barn. Grandpa followed. I tried to get where I could see, but Grandpa told me to get back and stay clear of the barn.

I didn't want them to do it. I was frightened for them, but more for the horse. I can't explain how I felt. I turned to Grandma, "Please, Grandma. Talk to him. Don't let him put that on the horse. It's torture, Grandma. Please, Grandma. That horse will learn to be better if they just let him be for a while. Please don't let them put that torture chamber on him." I was shouting.

Grandma ran her hand over my hair. "Janey, Janey. You know I can't tell your grandfather about horses. With Grandpa there is only one way for that horse to behave . . . or any horse, and that's *his* way, obediently. He doesn't care how or why the horse acts like he does. He's been breaking horses for so many years, he doesn't even think about it. A horse acts one way, and Grandpa acts another. It's like a rubber ball thrown against a sidewalk. It bounces. That's the only thing it can do, bounce. That's Grandpa and horses. There's nothing I can do to change it," she said quietly.

There was a stream of oaths from the barn. A crash as a bucket was kicked. Grandpa yelled, "Get that back door open!"

Seconds later the stallion emerged. He held his head high, ears erect. He shook his head as if to push away the piercing sunlight. Then I saw it. The chain was wrapped once around his neck and fastened with the snap lock. The log dangled in front of him, almost touching the ground. Grandpa came out of the barn, made a large circle around the stallion and opened the corral gate.

The big horse moved toward the gate. The log banged into his knees. He stopped. His head dropped for a moment under the weight of the chain and log. He lifted it again and took another step. His knees were smashed by the log again. He stood still. As if experimenting, he carefully turned his head to one side. The chain and log moved with it. He took a step. The log swung to the side. It did not hit his legs. He took another step, then another with his head in the same position.

He began a careful walk toward the gate. He walked through in this cattywampus posture with his head to one side. He was in the pasture and walking faster now, the log swaying threateningly but not striking his legs.

I wanted to cheer, I wanted to cry. So he had outsmarted the log chain temporarily. So what? How long could he do that funny walk?

I ran back to the house. I went upstairs to my room and into the closet. It was harder to get back into the roof-floor triangle now than it had been a few years ago. I went as far as I could and curled up with my knees at my chest. Downstairs I heard Grandma, Grandpa and Ed come in and have coffee. I didn't come out. Grandma called to me several times. I didn't answer. I didn't want to ride with Ed now. I didn't want to do anything.

The day passed slowly. It was hot and quiet in the closet. I thought about the stallion down in the pasture. In my imagination I planned schemes for taking the chain off and turning him loose. I imagined him so grateful for being saved that he became my friend and let me ride him. We would become famous in western movies. I would wear a shiny red cowboy outfit, the same color as my horse. My blonde hair would be very long, and brushed just like his mane and tail. We would perform everywhere, maybe for the Queen of England, and at lots of rodeos. The crowd would applaud and cheer as we rode into the ring. I would ride in a circle and wave my hat. They would introduce us with a drum roll. What would I name him? His father's name was Sunfish . . . Sun Dance? I knew! Fire Dancer. A perfect name for his color and spirit. *Sqreeeek* went a tree branch on the roof to remind me I was in the closet. I thought about what Ed had said about Mr. Gilmore and how he raised horses a special way so they would be mean. What would you do with a horse like that? Three horses killed themselves last year at the bucking horse sale. They bucked so hard and crazily they ran into the fence and broke their necks. Grandpa said it was better to have a place to sell horses like that than to send them to the glue factory because they were no good on a ranch. If a horse was mean and he couldn't be ridden, it's better he have the glory of the rodeo. But if Mr. Gilmore made horses mean so he could get more money for them as rodeo stock, what happened to them when they got too old to buck? I didn't know. It seemed pretty topsy-turvy.

When it became too hot and cramped in the closet, I went out into my room. There was a breeze coming in my window. My bed sheets felt cool and soft after the closet floor. I decided to lie down and read, but I fell asleep and dreamed of the big red horse. He was running and playing in the purple alfalfa. He chased rabbits and played like a puppy. I was laughing at his antics as I awoke. Grandma was calling me to supper.

No one said a word to me about my behavior. They were very polite. It surprised me.

During supper Grandma announced that she was low on everything and needed to go into town tomorrow. Grandpa said that was fine. He could use the trip to get some parts for the tractor. He wanted to get everything in shape before the haying started. Ed said he planned to spend the night and leave in the morning, early, to get into town before he had to be at work.

Nothing was said about the stallion that evening. We all went to bed early.

The Wait

Chores were done and breakfast out of the way very early. Grandpa got the car out of the garage. Ed left in his truck. We locked the dogs in the barn and drove out of the yard. The trip took about forty-five minutes, because Grandpa drove the old Plymouth very carefully on the bumpy gravel road.

Grandpa had on his navy blue suit pants and a white shirt. Grandma wore some gray slacks and a soft white blouse. Her hair was combed back in a neat roll at the nape of her neck, and she had put on some lipstick. She looked nice. I studied her profile as she turned her head to speak to Grandpa. Her nose was delicate and her eyes large. She was pretty. I wondered if I were pretty. I hadn't thought about it much.

In town, Grandma and Grandpa went to shop for groceries and tractor parts. I was free to wander on Main Street. I looked in the window of the J. C. Penney store. There were some brown leather loafers with an Indian Chief in a big headdress embossed on the toe. I wanted that style for my school shoes, but I wouldn't be able to get them until August. I hoped they would still have them in my size.

I strolled up the block to the dime store. This was the best store in town. It had toys and comic books and a soda fountain, but I liked the jewelry counter the most. There were flashing rhinestone pins and earrings and necklaces, gold and silver bracelets of varying shapes and widths. There was a glass case with several black velvet trays. The trays held hundreds of rings, rings with red stones, blue, green, pink . . . all kinds of rings. I loved to look at them. Once when I had some birthday money, I had gathered my courage and asked the clerk to bring out one of the trays and I tried on all the rings on the tray in my size. Not today, though. I had a dollar and I knew what I wanted. I was going to buy the new "Tales of the Crypt" comic book and save the rest of my money for the new headlight for my bicycle. The rings were a temptation, but I walked passed them and back to the comic book section. I found "Tales of the Crypt." It looked like a very spooky issue. I was about to go to the counter to pay for it when I saw the picture of a big red horse on the cover of one of the Western comics. I wondered where the stallion was. How far he got yesterday? How far *could* he go?

I paid for my comic and went looking for Grandma. She was putting the groceries in the car. She said that Grandpa had gone to the Range Riders for a beer and she wanted me to come with her to look at some dress material and choose a pattern. I wanted to go home right now, but Grandma insisted.

We went into J. C. Penney. I chose a dress pattern and some blue and white checked gingham as quickly as I could without seeming uninterested. While Grandma was paying for it, I suggested we get back to the car, in case Grandpa was waiting for us. Grandma looked at me curiously and asked if there was something wrong. I said no.

Grandpa returned to the car shortly after we did. We all piled in and started the drive back to the ranch. The road was very dusty. It didn't take long to dry out in these parts. We saw some antelope and two pheasants on the drive, but I didn't pay much attention. I was figuring how I could get a horse and sneak out to look for the stallion.

There was work to do when we got home. I helped Grandma put away the groceries and we had to make a nest for the setting hen. Grandpa hadn't closed the pasture gate this morning and the milk cows had gotten out. He asked me to go get them. I thought this would be an opportunity to go find the stallion. I asked if I should ride Blue or Smoky. Grandpa told me Smoky wasn't ready to ride yet, and I didn't need to take a horse because it was close to milking time and the cows would be heading toward the corral.

Grandpa was right. I took the dogs with me and found the cows just below the barn in the cottonwoods. They were on their way into the corrals. All I had to do was hurry them along with the dogs and a willow switch I picked up on the way. I delivered the cows to Grandpa for milking, then gathered the eggs. Suppertime. I would have to postpone looking for the stallion until tomorrow.

During supper I asked Grandpa if I could have a horse the next day to ride out and look at the new calves.

"Nope," Grandpa answered. "I told you, Smoky's shoulder is still healing. I'll have to take old Blue to ride to the upper pasture and check on the mares. We still don't know if there is a colt. I might even bring the mares on down to the corral. No. On second thought, I'm going to leave them up there until we get that stallion out of here."

Grandma said, "It appears that tomorrow will be a good day to start that new dress."

I didn't say anything. I was disappointed. I helped with the dishes and went up to bed.

Grandma let me sleep late the next day. When I came
downstairs, Grandpa was gone and she had cleared breakfast,
except for my place. The dress fabric was lying on the dining-
room table. Grandma's sewing box sat on the oak buffet. It
was a covered basket. The straw was a delicate weave which
had darkened with age. The basket was lined with wheat-gold
satin and filled with buttons from other worlds, rainbows of
thread and a pair of silver scissors shaped like a stork. His
beak parted to cut the thread. Usually I loved to sift through
the sewing basket, imagining the buttons on wonderful
dresses, playing with the colored thread. Today it didn't
interest me. Grandma, however, had decided that today was
the day I should start learning to sew. She coaxed me through
the laying out of the pattern on the fabric, explaining why
certain pieces had to go certain ways, the grain of the fabric
and all that. I wasn't paying attention. She repeated instruc-
tions, but I cut two pieces the wrong way. Then I basted
all the darts on the wrong side. By noon, Grandma was
thoroughly disgusted with me and suggested that I go and
read for the afternoon or something.

I went outside not knowing what I wanted to do. It was
hot, noon hot, and still, except for the buzzing of the flies
and the whir of the grasshoppers. This was not my favorite
time of day. Everything was heavier, as though the sun was
pushing down with the weight of its heat. I decided to go to
the river. It was cooler there.

The dogs came with me and played tag with each other in
the willows. I found the piece of window screen I kept
hidden under the fallen tree and waded out about knee deep
and seined minnows. Holding the edge of the screen with
both hands, I would put it underwater for a minute and pull
it out very fast. The small white fish would flop around on the

screen. I could look at them or hold them if I wanted, then let them go and seine some more. Once I tried to keep two of them in a bowl at the house. I brought new river water to them every day, but they died. I never tried to keep them again. It was enough just to be able to catch them.

When I grew bored with seining, I waded back in to the bank and looked for good flat rocks for skipping. I tossed rocks, I skipped rocks into the afternoon river. I threw sticks and watched them float away around the bend, on and on through the ranch. I bet the river knew where the stallion was. I wished that I could move through the ranch like the river.

The afternoon ambled by. I saw Grandpa, coming back from his ride. When he crossed the river I ran to meet him at the barn. As he unsaddled Blue he told me that the mare had not yet foaled, but it would be any day now. Then he said, "You know, I halfway expected I'd find that big red horse down there in the cottonwoods, but I didn't see a sign of him. Can't imagine where he is. I didn't think he'd get out of the cottonwood trees with that contraption on him. I think I'll take a look around the river bottom pasture tomorrow. You want to come along, Janey?"

"Yes!" I shouted.

Later, at supper, Grandpa told Grandma of our plans. She looked at us both with disapproval. "Janey, I thought you would have had your fill of that by now. You were upset for days and you're still not yourself. You didn't enjoy the trip to town yesterday, and you can't seem to concentrate at all. You certainly were miles away while we were trying to sew today."

"But Grandma, I couldn't concentrate because I was worrying about the stallion."

Grandpa laughed, "Janey, that is something. The stallion went after your hide a few days back, and now you're worried about him? He's so tough that we'll be lucky if we can load him *this* weekend."

Still, I couldn't wait until the next morning.

I got up and fed the chickens before breakfast to try to get on the good side of Grandma, who still didn't want me to go. After breakfast I helped her with the dishes while Grandpa saddled Blue and Smoky. As we rode out of the yard, the dogs scared up a rabbit and went yelping off, leaving Grandpa and me to ride out alone.

The morning was cool but it would be another scorcher by noon. We rode through the lower pasture toward the cottonwoods. Grandpa said, "Now keep a lookout. I imagine he'll be standing somewhere in the deep grass, probably not too far from the water so he can get his food and drink without much moving around."

We zigzagged back and forth through the lower pasture. There was no sign of the stallion.

Grandpa stopped and pushed his hat back. He wrinkled his forehead, bewildered. "This is strange. That horse didn't go through the fence. The fence isn't torn anyplace. Where could that son-of-a-gun be? Do you suppose that crazy horse crossed the river with that chain around his neck?" Then a smile, slow and disbelieving, spread across Grandpa's face. "Maybe he did. Maybe he did. Let's just take a little jaunt across the river."

We rode into the river at the crossing. It wasn't deep; belly-high, no more. On the other side we began our crisscrossing through that pasture. We covered this one quickly, as it was small. No sign of him here either. Grandpa insisted he had to be there. We crossed the pasture again. We covered every inch with either our feet or our eyes.

Grandpa stopped at the willows bordering the river. "Wait a minute," he said. "Let's ride along the bank here. Maybe he's hiding in a thick clump of willows right near the river."

We rode on the narrow strip of mucky land between the willows and the water. The willows slapped at my face and Blue slipped twice on the mud.

I saw him first. "Grandpa, Grandpa! Look!" I screamed. Standing in the river, halfway across, was the stallion. His back was toward our shore and his head hung down, his nose in the water. He lifted it slightly to breathe, then dropped it back again. His red coat was matted and streaked with mud. His tail hung limply in the water and he looked as though someone had taken out his padding, leaving his hide draped over bare bones.

Grandpa was amazed. "He was trying to get to the mares again. I don't believe it. He made the first river crossing into this pasture. But it looks as though he got hung up on the second crossing. I'll wade on out there and see if the chain is snagged on something. Isn't that something, though. If he had made it across this time, he *would* have been back up there with the mares. Never occurred to me that he'd try the river with that chain hanging on him."

Grandpa continued to exclaim as he removed his boots and dungarees.

Except when he lifted his nose to breathe, the stallion seemed dead on his legs. The water swirled by him, through his legs and away. Grandpa waded up to him. The stallion didn't move. Grandpa cautiously reached forward and grabbed the chain. It came readily out of the water. It wasn't snagged. Carefully, Grandpa reached under the big red neck and unfastened the snap lock. He turned and carried the chain and log back to the muddy bank. The stallion did not move. His nose dangled like a wet rag in the water. Grandpa swatted the matted red backside with his wet hand, *spat*. The stallion just stood there. Grandpa waded back to me.

"He looks bad. Might have been out there for a day or two. Probably left the corral and headed for the mares without stopping to eat. Started right back, then got out there and didn't have the strength to go any farther. Now he don't care if he gets out or not. I'm going out there with a rope and pull him out."

He took the lariat off his saddle and waded back to the stallion. He slipped a loop over the stallion's neck and braced his body against the current and pulled. The stallion didn't budge. Grandpa tried pulling from several different positions. The stallion was immobile.

Wet and muddy, Grandpa carried the end of the lariat back to the riverbank. The loop was still around the stallion's neck.

"Get off your horse," he ordered.

I got down. He turned Blue around, wrapped the rope around the saddle horn and tied it securely. Blue braced in the slippery mud, then strained forward. He slipped, righted himself, and pulled again. The stallion barely moved, but he had turned so he was facing downstream. Grandpa made Blue pull again. Blue's powerful forelegs reached, one then the other inched slowly forward on the slippery bank. And the stallion moved forward with him, then stopped and seemed to brace against the rope.

"Pull, Blue," shouted Grandpa. "That horse is still trying to win. Now he thinks he can just die on us in the river. Pull, pull, Blue!"

Blue strained heavily. His saddle tipped back under the strain. Grandpa urged him on. The stallion came slowly, step by step, toward the bank. His head dangled toward the ground, his proud neck limp. I could only stare. I saw the big red stallion's ghost, an airy figure with fierce eyes, his mane and tail floating like blond smoke, carried away in the current of the river, moving around the bend, rearing, flying, while the carcass was pulled up on the river bank like meat.

Grandpa got dressed. He removed the rope from Blue's saddle horn and told me to climb back on. He mounted Smoky, rode up beside the stallion and pulled the rope tight. He lifted the stallion's head with the rope, wrapped the rope around Smoky's saddle horn and set off at a walk through the willows, the stallion following on short lead.

My chest felt tight. My blood didn't seem to be going anywhere, just pumping and pumping. My heart, my throat were too full.

Grandpa put the stallion in a small corral. He told me to put Blue and Smoky in the barn. He would unsaddle them later. I saw Grandpa go for water and he had the oat bag with him.

Grandma was standing at the door of the house, waiting for me. "You found him?" she asked.

"Yeah, sort of . . ." I mumbled. There wasn't anything to say.

Grandpa gave the stallion a lot of attention for the next couple of days. He made special mixtures for him and rubbed him down with a rough blanket. I stayed to myself mostly and didn't go down near the corral or Grandpa much. I was glad he was taking good care of the stallion, but I didn't feel like being with Grandpa now.

Saturday, Mr. Gilmore came. I didn't see the loading of the stallion—I'd gone to the upper pasture to check on the mares.

I rode back over the places where only a week before the stallion had raged at me—hooves flashing, mane and tail waving like banners, wild and beautiful and frightening.

The mares were lying in the sun by the reservoir as I approached. They got up, stretched and sniffed the wind to see if they knew me. Then I saw him, standing beside a brown mare, still shaky on his legs, but curious. He walked out from behind his mother and stared at me. He was a deep auburn-red, with a white streak flashing down his nose. Fire Dancer!

I watched him for a few moments, then turned and galloped Blue back toward the gate. I couldn't wait to get home and tell everyone, to ask for this colt for my own, to *insist* that he be my horse, to be certain he had a place.